Also by the same
...ailable in

Josh Lawton

Melvyn Bragg

CORONET BOOKS
Hodder and Stoughton

First published in Great Britain by
Secker and Warburg Limited 1972

Coronet edition 1975
Third Impression 1978

The characters and situations in this book are entirely imaginary and bear no relation to any real person or actual happening

Printed and bound in Great Britain for
Hodder and Stoughton Paperbacks, a
division of Hodder and Stoughton Ltd.,
Mill Road, Dunton Green, Sevenoaks,
Kent (Editorial Office: 47 Bedford
Square, London, WC1 3DP) by
Richard Clay (The Chaucer Press), Ltd.,
Bungay, Suffolk

ISBN 0 340 19852 4

PART ONE

CHAPTER ONE

THEY could be seen together almost every evening of that spring on the high-fell road, and people would look out for them making their way back in the dusk, Cedric 'the trainer' leading on his motor-bike, the bright blob of his headlight a shifting beacon on the hillside, and behind him Josh, heavy boots tugging on the slim bare legs, intent on being trained.

'Breathe through your nose! Through your bloody nose to get cleaner air! Your nose strains it for you. Shut your effing mouth and breathe in; then open and blow. That's how they do it.'

Cedric would cut off the engine when they passed by cottages and farms, wanting his voice to be heard just as he gloried in being seen on his big motor-bike, black leather jacket, black boots and black gauntlets, preceding Josh along the bare hill road as special security police ride ahead of kings and presidents. He took all the care he could to keep an unvarying distance ahead of Josh, believing that in this gap lay some of his credibility as a trainer of athletes. It was difficult to do on that road which cut along the fellside: he had to swerve with the incline or against it and sometimes run up the verge, tack like a small yacht on a lake and then again press forward uphill at all but impossibly low speeds. No one appreciated the efforts he had to make.

Josh was easy to admire. Everyone knew he'd already done a day's work on the farm and when Wilson was your boss you worked. Yet here he was striding out, those big working boots hitting the road as if they had springs inside them, and always a smile if he passed you; a nice smile, no showing off about him. Cedric of course was painful the way he put it on, the way he played up, the way he acted big: and all he did was put his bum on that motor-bike! *He* could never run, couldn't run a raffle, but that didn't stop him shouting at poor Josh: all mouth—the Army hadn't knocked that out of him in twenty-five years. You'd have thought that twenty-five years would have got rid of it. Because he wasn't *really* tough—he'd a lot of show and there were some who took it seriously, but nobody important. He never tangled with the real cowboys.

It would be difficult to imagine Josh in a fight. So friendly and pleasant with everybody: never known a man so happy. Which showed, they said, you couldn't tell a thing from the way people were brought up because Josh had been given a hard time in that orphanage place—the 'Fellways Boys Home'—painful, really, the way that vicar had made him run around after him. Towards the end they'd stopped letting new ones go there and at the very end there was only Josh and the vicar and Mrs Morrison who cooked and kept things tidy. But of course the house was too big and you could see it was being ruined by being empty. It was a wonder the boy hadn't gone wild but he never complained, Mrs Morrison said.

The vicar wouldn't let him have anything to do with the village of course: Ullaby people weren't good enough for him and his lot. Orphan! The bare-faced cheek! But you could always tell that Josh wanted to talk to you; just the way he looked you could tell he was miserable to have nobody to talk to except that vicar.

He was just a decent, ordinary lad and wanted to work on a farm, nothing special. He left the place to be hired at Wilson's and the vicar had gone mad when he had said he wanted to live in at the farm. Came down to Wilson—and Wilson was religious himself, that was the funny thing, chapel not church but every bit as strict—down he'd come, the vicar, and bellow and bawl about being left on his own! A man of his age and in his position! The boy was right to get away from him: often Josh was so good-natured that he seemed to have no sense of his own good but that time he'd been right. He'd run away when the vicar came: run up into the fells like an outlaw.

Wouldn't come down, they said, until he was certain he could stay at the farm.

Wilson had said it was nothing to do with him, but he'd gone for this vicar on principle. What it came down to was that he should leave the boy alone to sort his own life out for himself and for all his spluttering the vicar did nothing but contradict that; for all his long sentences it was Josh he wanted back in Fellways to keep him company, for all his posh talk. You couldn't take him by force, though: and the boy was clearly unwilling to go back of his own free will.

There was talk of the vicar being 'funny' and interfering with the boy but this was false. Mrs Morrison who would never miss a trick knew that it was false and there'd never been any talk like that before. It was just that the old man seemed frightened to be left on his own. Mrs Morrison would tell how he kept all the lights on at night like a child and those who passed the Grange very late or early morning bore this out. And then he began to walk at night—through Ullaby, round the road which led from one small patch of cottages to another, passing farm gates, the two shops, the pub, the church, the post office, and then, as he grew more desperate, down from the fells into the small town of Thurston five miles away where he'd talk with the policeman on night duty and go back to the station with him for some tea.

It would have been easy, of course, to become too attached to Josh, everybody saw that. Blond he was, but not the thin, straggly fairness that becomes mousy—chunks of blond hair, wavy and heavy on his sweet, clear face which in feature and complexion was lovelier than any in the village. Ullaby people delighted in that; he was a matter of local pride. No matter how many hundredweight of mashed potatoes and turnips Mrs Wilson laid out for him, no matter how often he was out in bitter weather that chapped even old men and threatened a harvest of chilblains, no matter he was careless about bathing himself and rarely changed out of his working clothes—his complexion stayed unblemished. Older people would bring forward comparisons from their youth, those they had known, those they had heard of: it opened an uncommon vein of talk, this beauty of Josh's. Either you accepted it and treasured it or you would have to tease him about it and be rather embarrassed for the lad when girls came up and asked him what he used for his skin. But teasing hurt him so much—though he'd never complain he'd squirm like a ten-year-old and you could see the blood beating against his skin; and when the girls came up he was so open, so helpless in his inability to answer the question that you were left with a feeling of a rare manliness, just as after the teasing you were left with the impression of a rare modesty.

And Josh *was* a rarity, special in Ullaby. This small Cumbrian farming hamlet which clung to the side of the first rise of fells from the Solway Plain and looked down on the plain and over the firth to matching hills in Scotland, was inhabited by no more than half a dozen families—Josh's background was unknown. Everyone else in Ullaby was as rooted there as the yew tree which stood in what had been the Church of England churchyard before the church had been deconsecrated and turned into a barn by Oglonby. Someone had once muttered that it might be the oldest tree in the district: no one tried to confirm this in case it was not so—they preferred the safety of the muttered possibility. It was a poor village.

Josh stayed with Wilson and never asked for a change, endured the Methodist's sermons and severities and always appeared to be happy. That was what so distinguished him. For a time, many people in the village thought he was merely daft or had a nervous habit of smiling or was somehow afflicted: only slowly, only gradually, only through knowing him and seeing him closely day in day out for the five years he'd worked at Wilson's had people come to accept his happiness as something compatible with good sense and usefulness. There *was* something marvellous about him, something bottomless in his willingness to be of service; and just as his looks had brought out lengths of reminiscence and interest in beauty and a man's looks—whether a man *could* have good looks and what besides hair *was* the difference between the face of a man and that of a woman—so the transparency of his good nature brought out instances of goodness and godliness and neighbourliness. Josh became charmer and charm and even that did not ruffle him and even that did not spoil him nor turn them against him.

They would protect his reputation outside the village, speak up for him as for a favourite son when others teased or commented. In his small way then—for it must not be thought that Josh was a serious preoccupation in a place where snow could kill a flock of sheep and rain rot a harvest, where the huddle on the hillside drove people deep into their family and the usual twentieth-century wires made the usual twentieth-century connections—he was a wonder.

No doubt his talents helped disarm opposition and dispel doubts. At school—people remembered the one year when he had gone to Thurston school with the other children from the village; until then the vicar had insisted that 'his' children go in the other direction, to a village no bigger than Ullaby itself but one with a school which the orphanage had kept up—in class, Josh could be brought to tears by insistent questioning. He did not like to speak in public; he did not like to answer back; and many times he could not answer, was incapable of answering the simplest questions. Then, blond hair dishevelled, face rose-red, tears running uncontrollably down his face and yet his lips not trembling for there were no sobs—you could feel safe in calling him a dunce. But not outside the classroom. People knew that intelligence was involved in the body as in the brain, that skills of tying and ploughing, of caring for animals and gardening, of wrestling and building, these activities were just as difficult, just as complicated as paper work, though the world acted differently because those who ran it used the paper work to enforce their will. No one called Josh a fool who'd seen him mend a tractor; no one who'd watched him deal with a sick beast or a broken plough. No one, above all, who'd played any game with him, tried to wrestle with him Cumberland and Westmorland style, tried to beat him at any physical trick where the shrewdness of move and countermove combined with the gift of balance and strength to make his showing brilliant. But he did not take any sustained interest in sport—or had not done until Cedric's intervention—and people liked that, liked his carelessness about a talent which was, after all, of no use; liked the implied degrading of play in his scheme of things.

There had been one fight only and, though he scarcely

needed it, the event had clinched his popularity. For it had been a fight *about* the village at a sports meeting in Caldbeck—another, larger village, birthplace of John Peel, four miles away.

Ullaby had entered a football team for a five-a-side and got to the final where they had been beaten by a vehemently disputed penalty. Josh had not taken part in the arguing or barging: he played forward and had been far from the scene of the foul. He'd sat down and watched—wanting the incident to be over so that they could get on with the game and win it. He had scored in every round but seemed to have lost his touch here, in the final, when it most mattered. The other team got a goal from the penalty, the final whistle went soon afterwards, the players left the pitch. They went to a hedge in the corner of the large field. Here a couple of stacks of bales offered a screen while they changed and here the argument between two of the Ullaby players and the other team continued and grew worse, more bitter and, despite occasional soothing noises from some on both sides, more threatening. Josh, they said, ignored it all at first, dressing slowly and self-absorbedly as he always did, abstracting himself from this shuffling of limbs and teasing of privates, as he always did. Until someone from the other team had begun to accuse Ullaby, the village, to decry it, and using this entry as an excuse began to reduce and mock those who lived there. Ullaby people were . . . Ullaby women were . . . Ullaby was well known for . . . It was a form of abuse which bordered on being a joke depending on how you were prepared to take it: because the Ullaby men liked to believe that Ullaby men *were* . . . *did* have distinctive ways and were a tribe; they were even prepared to be abused (mildly) in order to have that confirmed. But there was unease because the tongue was bitter; and unremitting.

Josh warned him when he began to revile the vicar. He was an embarrassment, the man said: if he hadn't been a vicar they'd have taken him away. Only his dog-collar saved him from the madhouse. Josh warned the mocker but the man continued and with no second word, Josh hit him: friends went to his aid but before anyone from Ullaby could step in on Josh's side to even up the odds, they too were down—three of them—stunned by what had caught them.

The story was elaborated many times and at great length with Josh described as a 'madman', a 'whirlwind'—they said he had stood over them steaming with anger, that no one had been able to talk to him all night, that everyone was afraid to touch him to ask him to come away and the three floored men were too scared to get up, that he could not feel pain in such a mood and had a right fist which could break a door-panel, that you must never, never, rouse his temper.

Ullaby was deeply pleased.

And all this made his involvement with Cedric difficult to comprehend. They had been pals for about six months now and people were no nearer to understanding it than they had been at its beginning: but they had come to accept it, become used to the sight of the two of them together, even this 'training' was a matter they were greeting with no surprise. And Josh had not changed at all: he never would, they assured each other, devoutly.

'Pick up those effing legs! Up-two-three-four! Up-two-three-four! Do some of them chest presses at the same time. Press-press-press-fling! Up-two-three-four! Press-press-press-*fling*! We're nearly home now—come on, stop effing playing about! Now a sprint. To that corner. Wait till I'm ready. Now! Wait! Effing bike! Bloody machine! Wait! Josh! Just to that corner. This bloody rotten sod of a bike! Josh—wait on, eh? Josh? Josh!' But the younger man ran on and turned the corner.

Cedric was as open to the gossip of the village as Josh was closed to it. He heard the love for his new friend purring from cottage to cottage, he heard it in his head as clearly as he heard the chat about himself—that funny Cedric Tyson.

Forty. Forty years old, and twenty-five of them in the Army: joined the Boys' Army just before the end of the war. Every leave-time he came back to Ullaby where he'd been born and bred and brought nothing for his mother though she put him up and lived in bad health on a widow's pension. He'd never been much liked. Of course, the lads wanted to hear his stories—and could he tell them! The one about the whore of Singapore! One thing about Cedric, he could talk. But if you believed what he said about himself—well why hadn't he been promoted? And he would never do a hand's turn on any of those long holidays they give them in the Army: even that time he'd been back for three months after the Far East with one hell of a fight for any hay at all—he'd never done a hand's turn. There was something about him that the more respectable people in the village instinctively shrank from: he liked to taunt them occasionally by sinking deeper into that attitude, a combination of surliness and menace which they never thought to excuse by shyness as in others they would—because of Cedric's talkativeness. (Silence was much more admired; and more common thereabouts.) That in itself was all right in a steady married man: but such a tongue in the mouth of a man still unsecured—there was something untrustworthy in it. Why *hadn't* he got married? There were other bachelors about, true, many a hired man on those islanded fell farms was bred to bachelordom, it seemed, but Cedric was for ever telling of the women he'd had in Hamburg and Gibraltar and elsewhere—wasn't anybody in the village good enough for him? He never tried, it seemed. The women very soon came to suggest it might be because he knew they would never have him.

And take his language—it was a clean-mouthed community and though Cedric did his best it was not good enough. It was all very well to say 'effing' instead of the real thing: all very well to say that you were so used to it in the Army you couldn't stop though you would clean it up for the village and train yourself to say 'effing': but everybody knew what 'effing' meant and it was just as uncomfortable. He needed a mouth-wash: in disinfectant. Nor could you be sure of the rest of his words because he'd lost the Ullaby twang, no doubt of that: he spoke a much more 'proper' English than any of his former friends—than almost anyone in the village where the speech was clear through the slowness of the delivery rather than the purity of the language—but somehow it was odd. Though there was still a Cumbrian accent in it—especially when he was angry—it seemed to slip from place to place and never sounded as if it fitted his mouth properly, like slack false teeth.

What did you make of a man, though, who got his lump sum from the Army after his twenty-five years (*and* a bit of a pension—he would never say what) and spent most of it on a brand new motor-bike with all the latest fittings and a black leather jacket and boots and all the gear just to wear for riding it? He could have bought that cottage of his mother's for the money and saved paying rent ever again. Then there was that job of his at the quarry: what sort of work was it, anyway, driving a truck after all that army experience? You didn't need to have been to Singapore to drive a truck-load of granite. No, there was something very funny. There were men of his age in Ullaby, with grown-up sons and daughters, one was even a grandfather—and here was the bold Cedric buying special Japanese mirrors for a motor-bike.

In his own way, Cedric was as odd as Josh. But of course he was much more rooted in the village. Though far less well liked, he was more a part of the village than Josh. He would know whose back door was open to whose best foot when Josh would still be thinking about a good dinner he'd enjoyed. His mother's ill-health was nursed by village talk and Cedric had been brought up in forests of chat and rumour. The village was his mother's salvation in this world and she beat the drum and shook the tambourine. He was glad to get away from it, into the Army . . . Private Tyson, yes sir! But it was his body of knowledge, the present history of this village, it was the lining of information in his mind, the well of comfort he could and did draw on in those fearful days abroad. A very short time was needed to bring him up to date, and then he would begin to stir in his own powders.

Cedric had considered Josh a long time, on many leaves, before making the move towards a real friendship. He'd been disappointed too often before: he'd come on leave flush with money and willing to mate up with anybody, paying for this and that, left, right and centre and then something would go wrong and he'd be on his own again or merely part of the gang: the village gang, the men of Ullaby, boys in their teens, young men, bachelors and occasional grass widowers moving around like a small, somehow depleted unit. And Josh was so admired, so loved that Cedric could not help hating him. He had stirred his mockery into the common chat but it had been rejected and slapped him in the face. He had chafed Josh himself but found that the young man had in his mind a filter as strong as any portcullis and what he did not want to hear he appeared not to hear and what he did not want to wound him was glanced aside, no harm done. Nor any offence taken. Cedric was dismayed to discover that however hard he attempted to dent Josh's self-possession and his reputation the man would still greet him with the same smile the next time. Cedric seized on that for a while and tried to prove that all of Josh's character was based on an elaborate trick designed to disarm everyone, no matter who, by this incessant smiling. It was meaningless, Cedric maintained. But people would not listen: they knew that Josh had likes better and likes worse, it was difficult to discover someone he disliked but he'd never forgiven the man who had spoken against the vicar after the football match: they had met once or twice since and Josh had just walked away. He liked things, though; he liked the weather whatever it was and the way you were, he liked to do what you wanted and would listen to you: he just got up every morning and liked what he saw. People enjoyed Cedric's bewilderment.

Cedric had left him alone for a while.

In his bedroom—the door he secured with a double lock he'd fitted on himself—was Cedric's Empire. The walls were a mind-swirling montage of heroes and heroines, faces and bodies carefully cut out of shiny magazines and glued on to the uneven surfaces—athletes, body-builders, models, champions of motor-bike and racing-car, film stars, footballers, famous personalities—faces and limbs everywhere, sometimes three or four layers deep where he'd found new idols and been forced to cover the old. Sometimes he'd just lie on the bed and look around for hours, try to pretend he was going out with some of these people, what they'd say, what he'd do, where they'd go. He could have a good laugh sometimes when he'd think of things that could go wrong. Or he'd read, in this room, one of his war books perhaps and not feel exposed as he'd often felt in the barracks nor yet lonely because of all the familiar faces that would do as he wanted. And outside, there was a place where he knew everybody: every single person. Knew all about them. Nothing they could do without his getting to know about it sooner or later. Nothing!

This Josh, he was no part of the real village. Scarcely known there before he'd been hired by Wilson. And he could tell you a tale or two about *that* Methody sod!

Sometimes in his mind he would machine-gun the entire village. Line them up against the chapel wall like Al Capone's gang on St Valentine's Day and fill them with lead.

What he liked was to walk through the village in his new gear, feel the boots heavy and weighted on his feet, hands safe and protected in gauntlets, the soft (best) leather collar waxy against his burrowing chin and *feel* the place stir a little uneasily at his passing. Yes, though he knew them so well and they him, he could still brush the hairs the wrong way. His absences had intensified this power which, he felt, he'd always had, to disturb the village and make it wonder. How he could hate the place! If only they knew how he could hate that grey cluster of cottages and farms plastered on a fellside, no more dignified than gatherings of scree or a stack of rocks, that tight little Ullaby where everybody was in and everything came out. Sometimes, away from it, he would be happy just in that—that he was away; and he'd go through the villagers name by name, calling them to his mind mockingly, and threateningly.

His mother never said a word to him about the way he behaved but he knew she complained to others. He had begun to give her something every week now that he was back permanently. When he'd been on leave he'd needed all the money for himself: it was his holiday, after all; he had worked for it. She was his mother, after all: she could not begrudge him bed and breakfast. He was a light eater.

He had met Josh one night at the crossroads where they all went at some time or other of a night and found himself talking of systems and programmes. That was what you picked up in that Army—ways to talk like that and know what you were about. Besides, he was interested: that's why he'd gone into the Army in the first place. Who wanted to be stuck on a farm all their lives? He had plans. He would travel. Watch out.

Carried away by the flawlessness of Josh's attention, Cedric had spun into a torrent of false statistics, lying claims, boasts, proofless instances and emphatic promises. Josh had been saturated. And he was much impressed. Cedric—an ordinary Ullaby lad—to have done all these things, gone to the Middle East and what not, all over. *He* wouldn't have gone abroad for a fortune: literally not. Thurston and Keswick were far enough: even Carlisle was a struggle—he wanted to be out of that strange, crowded city where you saw no one you knew and so soon felt isolated and at the same time crowded out. He could not fathom it—did not try to. How much further than that had Cedric gone! Yet with all his experiences, with all his knowledge of other countries and other peoples, with all those languages he could rub along in and all those customs he knew, with all the interesting people he must have met and all the interesting people around there were to talk to—here he was, spending all this time with him. Josh was flattered and, sensing that, Cedric let go the fascination he had been holding back, released the feeling he had for this younger man and welcomed the friendship.

The training had started from talk about fell-racing—running up a mountain and down again—and the money to be won from the bookies if an outsider could come in and win a big meeting. There would be long odds on an unknown. And Cedric would keep him unknown; would take him only on those lonely paths the huntsmen followed for their sport.

Josh had willingly said he would give it a try and the harmless surprise, as he saw it, in the enterprise even carried him over the embarrassment of running around the fell-roads after Cedric's motor-bike. He still refused to trot through the village in his shorts (Cedric had got these for him: black) and insisted on changing back into his jeans before re-entry just as he stipulated that Cedric give him a lift out of the village on the pillion to a place where he could change and then begin. The nature of the deal was the thing which made the relationship between the two men palatable to the rest of the village. After all, Cedric might be on to a good thing (he'd been known to be lucky before) and Josh certainly *did* have the makings of a runner: when Cedric entered him for a race he would let them all know —he had promised that—and they'd all be able to get a bet on. It could make the village rich. Of course the Methodists would not gamble: but neither would they be spoilsports; they would like to see their local lad whip those well-known runners. He could, no doubting that.

See how he ran!

Josh had taken advantage of Cedric's trouble with the bike to get a long lead. It was not often he got a chance to play a trick on his trainer. The difficulty, on these fell-roads, was finding somewhere to hide: they were so bare.

He came to the place where the track turned off up to the quarry. Cedric drove up there and around the side of the fell every working day in his truck: it was gutted by the twin wheel-ruts: shifting with mud. How he would hate to bring his spotless motor-bike up there! But how much more he would hatc to walk!

Josh ran up the track to where it turned sharp left and followed the side of the fell. There, at the elbow bend, was an abandoned building, once the storehouse and offices of the many iron-ore workings which had so recently pocked the hill-sides. It was built rather like a small castle, this place, crenellation, narrow windows (no glass left), something romantic about it. Josh went inside and stood on a pile of broken wood to look through the window and through the dusk to the road where Cedric would not be looking for him.

In many tones his name was cried out: 'Josh!' 'Josh?' 'Jo-osh.' 'Josh!!' In anger, frustration, misery, agitation, as a question, an exclamation, a plea—but however it came it stung Josh with pleasure, the sound of it. The massive headlight swept the fellsides, stroking the wet bracken, and the throbbing beat of the big engine claimed echoes from the hills and still Josh didn't stir until at last Cedric swung the headlight on to the building and Josh ducked.

'I know you're there, you effing bastard! Come on! Come on! I'll make you run till you're sick! Come on out! Josh! Josh! I'm warning you!'

He revved up the machine and it roared and roared again at the silence of that dusk-felted darkness. Josh shouted back at it, unable to contain himself any longer. 'Come and find me! Come and find me! Where am I? Eh?'

Slowly the black machine came up the track, carefully steered between the ruts and from being a spread light on the fell the circle crept inwards and concentrated only on the building. The noise was tremendous out there among the empty, echoing fells and when he reached the place, Cedric pushed the special horn he'd bought which was supposed to make the sound of a New York Police Siren.

Josh came out with his hands up, smiling mischievously.

Cedric knocked off the engine and the light.

The dark and the silence were sudden and strange between them.

CHAPTER TWO

Josh shared a bedroom with Norman, the other hired man. Mrs Wilson had once offered to clear an attic room and put a bed in it for him but Josh preferred to share. He liked the cosiness of it and Norman's chat in the half-light when each was in his bed. Between the two single beds was a length of coconut matting and a table for the alarm clock and their valuables. They shared a wardrobe but each had two drawers to himself in the chest and there was a chair each for dumping clothes on. Norman painted the room out each spring, this time in pale blue. The walls were unadorned: Mrs Wilson disapproved of ornament.

Norman had been with Wilson for twelve years. A man of forty-three, he was known to be only a fair worker, nothing exceptional, but a particularly cheerful sort of fellow: Wilson's constant gloominess obviously found some relief in Norman's good temper and he was less hard on him than he had been on other men. Nor was he too hard on Josh now; Wilson was not one who could bully just for the sake of it and after many months' tyranny which provoked none of the reactions and gave none of the satisfaction he had hoped for, he had accepted the boy as someone he could like as well as defend. Norman and Josh did all the heavy jobs: Wilson was gradually running down the farm; the arthritis in his hands prevented him from doing much serious work.

Josh liked to lie in bed, stare at the ceiling and just be there. Sometimes they said nothing—that was the beauty of it, there was nothing forced. Norman liked to smoke in bed and, as Mrs

Wilson had forbidden it, they kept the window open and the older man would blow his smoke at the black framed space. To give himself some home comfort, Norman had bought a side-light because he enjoyed a read with his last cigarette and hated having to get up and walk over the cold, rough coconut matting to put out the light at the door. His greatest pleasure was to snuggle under warm clean flannel sheets—Mrs Wilson did you well in bedding, just as she could not be bettered for her feeding and her laundry—to burrow in there with his legs tucked up—he'd never lost that childish habit—and smoke a cigarette while he read a magazine, *Reveille*, *Weekend*, anything like that: pictures of blondes in bathing-suits and articles on peculiar subjects like second sight, witchcraft, hypnotism, that sort of thing which gave you a small shiver and also a subject of interest.

Josh being there was just the very item that topped his pleasure up. Norman had been brought up in a large family and even in his first years as a labourer he had not had a bed to himself. He remembered the night he'd first slept alone in a bed designated for his sole use; it was a well-remembered occasion and an achievement. Of course, it was surprising how soon times changed, he would never share a bed now, this last half-hour at night was far too precious and the total rule he enjoyed over the kingdom of that bed was very much part of his happiness. But he would have been lonely without someone else in the room—he liked to be able to look up and talk to somebody. One of the reasons for his poor reputation as a worker was that he disliked working on his own and would botch many a lonely job through hastiness: at those times he would find himself talking to himself and that caused a strain in his mind, he said.

He would put the light on the floor so that he got only a soft effect on his page. He did not believe in reading in a hard artificial light; he had read somewhere that it was bad for the eyes. Projected on to the ceiling would be the pattern from the top of the shade and drifting through it the smoke from the illicit cigarette.

Josh would lock his arms behind his neck, stretch out his legs until his heels rubbed on the bottom corners of the mattress, then with his toes lift up and then lower the flannel sheets so that a slight draught ran over his bare skin and quickly snuffed out. He liked to stare at the patterns on the ceiling, particularly contented on nights when he had come in from training and the night gave way to the dusky room, the fierce headlight to the soft sidelight, Cedric to gentle Norman.

Josh, too, considered himself to be fortunate. 'I've nothing to worry about,' he had assured Cedric. 'Wilson takes off my tax, he takes off for my stamp and he puts a pound a week in the post office for me. So when I collect my envelope, it's all mine, all there is in it. Mrs Wilson gets all the meals, does all my washing, buys me things she thinks I want. I've never any worries.'

He liked best the time when Norman nicked his cigarette, popped it out of the window, shook the curtains before drawing them to clear them of smoke, and then switched off the light.

They were always silent for the first few moments.

That night Norman did not read for as long as he usually did; wanting the light off so that he could once more whet his curiosity about Cedric.

'So you're serious about this fell-racing then, eh?'

'Oh yes.'

'Tell me, what d'you make of Cedric?'

'I like him.'

'I know that. But what sort of a man *is* he?'

'He's all right.'

'I know that, Josh, but is he a difficult sort of a man or an easy sort of a man?'

'He's easy to get on with.'

'To you, yes, granted. Because you can give him something, see. But what's he like to everybody else? That's my argument.'

'He seems all right.'

'Some say he's very—funny, a funny sort of a man. I mean, that new motor-bike at his age.'

'He likes it.'

'Granted. We all like something. But it's such a flash job. And it'll just get knocked to bits on these roads, I can tell you that.'

'We should start on that top pen tomorrow. Wilson says he

wants it mended.'

'I was talking about this friend of yours.'

'It needn't take two of us. Would you like to go on your own or should I?'

'Both! We both need to go. It's hard work lifting those stones, lad. It needs us both.'

'All right.'

Norman paused, grateful to be rescued from the prospect of spending hours alone high up the fell rebuilding a stone sheep-pen, and yet again irritated—baffled by that point in Josh which simply could not be touched.

'When he doesn't want to hear he doesn't hear,' Norman would relate, 'and what he doesn't want to see he's blind to; and same with everything. Sometimes I think he's got something we haven't got, other times I think he must be lacking.'

Josh lifted the sheet with his toes and let the draught in.

'I wish there was rain outside,' he said, 'a storm. I like being in bed then.'

So did Norman, loved to snuggle deep into his warm bedding. But, to punish Josh, he did not agree with him.

'Listen,' said Josh.

Norman held his breath: the silence kneaded into his ears; he saw in his mind the fells outside, mile on mile of bare hillside and everything so empty; Ullaby only a few dwellings clinging to the fellside, no more than the broken sheep-pen.

'What is it?' he asked, a little tremulously. He had frightened himself by 'seeing' outside.

'Your blood. You can hear it going round.'

'*You* can maybe. Mine's a quieter lot . . . Anyway, what do you want to listen to your blood for? Something to do with what Cedric says about this training?'

'No.'

'You'd better watch out this training doesn't bring on a seizure.'

Josh did not reply but Norman heard the long sighing yawn as the body stretched itself contentedly in the darkness.

'You can laugh. It's these fellows go hunting every day—they can do fell-running, they've built up the heart and the legs and the lungs for it. Lads like you'll just collapse in a heap.

You'll drop.'

'You haven't been on a hunt lately, Norman.'

'No.'

'You used to go a lot.'

'I did! I was keen. You're right! I did. Yes.'

It was a matter of some bitterness to Norman this hunting—hunting, on foot in the fells. There had been a disagreement over a subscription. Norman said he had paid it and the treasurer could find no record. Instead of accepting his loss in good faith and with good humour, the treasurer persisted in coming up to Norman every single time he saw him and bellowing, 'Are you *sure* you haven't remembered?' The more he shouted the more obstinate Norman became, and the more the treasurer shouted. This trouble had begun the previous autumn and Norman had gradually become sickened of attending meets with that pack. He missed it badly.

'I was doing too much anyway. It was keeping me from other things.'

The young man made no immediate effort to quench the silence. Eventually, he said: 'Isn't it great just to lie here in comfort and listen.'

'To what?'

Josh did not reply. Norman waited and then heard the long steady breaths of sleep.

Fully dressed, Cedric lay on his unmade bed and stared up at the light bulb. He had changed to go down to the pub, taken off his leather jacket and boots and substituted a sports jacket and shoes. There were times when he enjoyed provoking a response and times when he wanted the centre of attraction to be someone else. He went to the pub to talk over the day and wanted to be incognito; like a VIP.

He had drunk three bottles of Guinness as always. Guinness, he maintained, was not really like drinking. It had building properties. A doctor had told him that once, in Aden, when he'd been convalescing and needed building up. He did not smoke. Though no athlete himself, he liked to keep in shape and did twelve push-ups first thing in the morning and last thing at night. Sometimes he would spend all of a Saturday afternoon on a work-out in his bedroom, doing all the exercises he had been drilled into in the Army. The Army did not keep you as fit as people thought: you ate too well.

He patted his hair as he lay on the bed, felt over it with his fingers. No one knew. He had spotted the signs of baldness early on and decided to catch it there and then. No expense spared. New hair thatched in. Gradually. Went to a place in London—in Soho, a friend had got him the address—and had it replaced as necessary. All the top of his head was now new hair and they'd said the back and sides would not go bald. So he was safe. It had cost seventy-four pounds in all. He was proud of his extravagance and of his ability to pay. In Ullaby they wouldn't pay three and six for a haircut. He trimmed his back and sides himself with the help of a three-piece mirror he had bought in Aldershot. No one had ever guessed. No one knew. Not even his mother.

There had been something in the pub, some gesture, some remark which now rose into his mind; something dismissive or disparaging, in some way insulting . . . Patiently he went over the conversation, trying to picture who had been there; trying to remember what had been said or done. He was not very good at recalling such things but he was persistent, when he wanted something that he thought he could get he was persistent. He never gave up. Like the Royal Canadian Mounted Police, he always got his man! He liked to think of himself as a Mountie sometimes; at other times he was Robert Mitchum. There weren't any real tough guys on the pictures any more. Or he was that soldier in *The Naked and the Dead*—he'd seen the film four times and read the book.

What was it?

They'd been talking about training and he'd been telling them about the way Emil Zatopek trained and Gordon Pirie and Herb Elliot—and there'd been this argument about whether Herb Elliot trained on hard sand or on soft sand, whether he did his running on the flat beach or in the dunes . . . maybe one in the mornings and the other at night, maybe one for one type of training and the other for another, maybe both, perhaps neither—it could have been a publicity stunt, this sand, they said.

Cedric *knew*, of course. He was absolutely one-hundred-per-cent certain of the correct answer but there was no convincing them. He *knew*. He was indisputably right and he knew ten times as much about all this as the rest of them put together. He *knew*. They were getting at his own training methods for Josh but he did not let that rattle him, just kept on calmly, that was it, calmly telling them what was right. They didn't know a thing in this hole, this dump, this one-eyed crummy tenth-rate nowhere of a place. This, this dead-from-the-neck-up, US-in-the-last-century joint, this stupid herd of sheep-shaggers (Sergeant-Major Watson had called *him* that). But he'd kept his temper. Just pointed out that as a matter of fact he *knew* that the Australian miler Herb Elliot ran in the effing sand-dunes morning and night and that was that. He would discuss it of course but there could be no argument. Because he was right. I mean, they could have their point of view, everybody had a point of view, but not on facts. Facts were outside of argument. So they could argue but it made no difference because he *knew*. He didn't have to prove it. Didn't need to. It stood by itself. But they would never listen to him, and so in his head had been the pulsing black tremor of fury which he dare not release. Those suppurating and suffocating swellings of emotion which literally seemed to beat against the bones of his brow, strain against his ear-drums, pour into his neck, make him fear to choke, afraid to sip the beer even for some minutes in case he could not swallow. Even now, on the bed, just recollecting it, his head grew hot with anger at the memory of it. He had wanted to hit out but was afraid, he told himself, to cause trouble and anyway it was such a small matter and they were so obviously so wrong. *Every*body knew Herb Elliot's training methods! For Christ's sake! It had been all over the bloody papers all the bloody time and he, Cedric Tyson, had once docked at Darwin, Australia, and had thirty-six hours shore-leave, how the hell could anybody argue with *that*!

But that's what they did, in this place, just to get at him; precisely what they did. Because none of them had the guts to go further than Carlisle without running back to their mothers or their families.

Calthwaite! That was it. Bobbie Calthwaite had given him

the V-sign and pretended to disguise it by lifting a cigarette to his mouth at the time he did it. He had seen it and chosen to repress it, afraid to meet the challenge. Calthwaite had kept on giving him the V-sign every time he took a puff. All right if somebody did it openly—but that way: with everybody knowing except him! Calthwaite was a sod! All that time he'd been seriously discussing athletics. Everybody smiling to themselves. Calthwaite was a flat-faced, squint-eyed, snotty-nostrilled—he took great care with these private oaths, and great care and great pleasure as they exploded inside his mind, blasting their objective to kingdom-come; there had been some *real* cursers in the Army, if you wanted to hear cursing, *really* nasty, just go in the Army—Calthwaite would have been an effing twat if he'd had anything at all between his legs: Calthwaite should be done.

As he did his push-ups, he concentrated on *how* he would get him.

CHAPTER THREE

THE snow came back and there could be no training. Cedric was glad when he saw it in the morning. Josh's fidelity to the course was much more enduring than his own. 'We'll have a treat,' he said, aloud, as he shovelled the greasy breakfast into his mouth. 'A change is as good as a rest. We were getting stale.' He grinned at his mother, wanting to incite her curiosity so that he could play with it; but she knew his games and shuffled in and out of the back-kitchen silently, huddled in shawl and slippers, her coat over her nightdress, the smell of her bed and her lotions competing with the tang of old cooking fat. Cedric forked a slice of fried bread and held it up: dripping ran off it, a steady trickle. 'What's this supposed to be! Eh! It'd clog a bloody tractor up, never mind a rotten man.' But the thought of an evening free made him too pleased to be convincing. 'I run my bike on less oil than this,' and he shook the bread before taking it in his hand and eating it.

The snow came down sporadically throughout the day. Enough stayed on the ground to make a new landscape of it, to mark out the hedges as bare black barricades wanting a purpose, to hide the walls on the fells and make the hills themselves puffed smooth and innocent-looking.

'Put a coat on.'

'I don't like them.'

'I'm not having you catch soddin' double pneumonia just when you're gettin' into shape. And it's freezin', for Christ's sake!'

Josh stood shivering, his hands in the pockets of his jeans, the old sports jacket buttoned up, a frayed blue shirt open at the neck. They were outside the gate of the farm.

'Put—a—bloody—coat—on.' Cedric was very pleased with Josh's obstinacy, it was yet another certainty about him; 'he'll never wear a coat; never.' Yet he thought that he, Cedric, could *make* him wear one.

'Look, Cedric, if we're gonna go, let's go. I'm perishin'.'

'You'll turn into an effing ice-block on the back of this bike.' He let there be a silence and watched the young man jog up and down. 'And those wellingtons are no protection. You need to look after your feet now, you know.'

Josh nodded and continued to jog about, waiting for this to be over. The dramatic force of such a silence diminished rather than grew as it lengthened, for Josh had lost interest.

'There's a coat in this side-bag.' Realizing that Josh would not willingly get it out, Cedric undid the bag and pulled out an army greatcoat which he carried for emergencies. He threw it at Josh, thus compelling him to catch it and so to accept it. 'I don't want you to be laid up,' he added, in a tone at once gruff and sly: for he did care about Josh's well-being and he wanted to impose his will on the younger man—yet he knew that a great weakness of Josh's was his politeness: and you could not refuse what had been given with such apparent generosity.

'Come on, old son. We'll be due back before we get there at this rate.'

Josh put on the coat and climbed on to the bike.

'Where're we going?' he shouted.

'I know a spot.'

Cedric had planned it all day, rejecting obvious places. He would let Josh have two halves of bitter, maybe three. The snow was set for a day or two and there could be no training while it lasted. He had chosen a pub in a village near Lake Bassenthwaite. He would never have gone there in summer—too crowded with people he feared and disliked. But it should be empty at this time, he thought, and he admired the class of the place, the oak beams and the carpets.

He drove carefully. The bike could make a great deal of noise but it was only rarely that he opened it up—and then the road had to be clear and the going good.

Through the snow-bound fells they went; farms cuddled by those creamy heaps of new flakes, shining under the rising moon, sheep bleating in their folds, no stir on the slopes; through villages where a handful only would be settled in a small pub for the night, Josh still with hands in pockets, gripping with his knees alone.

In the bar there were only three others—young people in sweaters and jeans and heavy expensive walking-boots, two men and a girl; Cedric guessed they were in their early twenties. He took their drinks to a table well away from them—even though this meant being far from the open log fire.

Josh was overawed, glanced around apprehensively and sipped little mouthfuls. Cedric took courage from this and stilled the flicker of anxiety which the presence of those others had set off. 'It reminds me of a place we used to go to in Salisbury,' he said, not quite whispering. 'Near the Cathedral—I went in there once, but there was a service on. And this pub was called The Cathedral, get it? So when I asked directions first time I landed up at the church instead. The highest spire in England—you should see it, Josh. I mean, Carlisle Cathedral's not a patch on it. Nowhere near. And it has lawns, this spot, a wall round it, tennis courts round the back, you know, for those that work there, vicars and their wives—it's very famous. It's probably the most famous in England outside London. I mean, you don't get bus-loads coming to Carlisle, do you? But in Salisbury—well—I tell you—at weekends we would have to walk in the gutters to let the tourists have the pavement. Always give way when you're in uniform—it creates a better impression. That's what we're told anyway. So this pub—bloody great fire—two, no three or four times the size of that thing over there, logs on it the size of tree-trunks—and carpets! You know a soldier's boot?—you know the regulation British Army boot?—well, those carpets came up and over that rim just up from the sole. Mind you, it cost you a bit—you could easily pay three bob, sometimes more, just for a sandwich. I tell you. In Singapore you could buy the whole effing pub for three bob! Eh?' His voice was loud now as he relaxed and felt the easing of pain which was the blessing Josh brought him; the chance to find ease for that pain which had grown on him all his life, become as a hunchback's hump on his spirit, and here was salved in the soft wax of this man's impressionable attention. 'Take your coat off, Josh, you'll miss the benefit when we come to go if you don't.'

The three strangers heard the instruction and smiled among each other as Josh stood up to obey. Cedric had his back to them, but Josh caught the interchange.

'It's a bit too flash for me, this place,' he said, and took a large mouthful of beer this time, all but emptying the glass. 'Maybe we could move on.'

'No—not a bit. You've got to learn about this sort of thing, Josh—be at your ease. That's what you get out of the Army, see? I'm at *my* ease anywhere you could mention. I know what to say and what not to say, how to dress——'

'I should've dressed up a bit more for here, that's what I think,' said Josh, forcing a rare interruption.

'No—not for a public bar, Josh. And not mid-week. And not in this kind of weather. You're OK as you are. AI.'

Josh nodded and was silent; he felt the weight of the curiosity of the others pressing on him but he did not want to argue aloud with Cedric. They drank for a time without talking.

'Another?'

'It's my round.'

'No. Trainer treats on nights off. Eh?' He took the glasses and went over to the bar, banging the bell a little over-emphatically to call back the barman from the saloon. Again Josh saw the interchange of smiles, this time directed against Cedric who, to Josh, looked very smart, leaning against the counter so casually in his expensive leather outfit. As he turned to bring back the drinks, one of the men, the taller one in a russet sweater which matched his hair, called out:

'Good evening.'

Cedric nodded, happily, and the froth bobbed in the clutched glasses.

'We were wondering if you could help us,' the man continued as Cedric walked from bar to table full of concern over the beer, terribly conscious of the carpet. Josh sensed they had *not* been wondering anything like that. While easily gulled in his relaxed submission to one he was prepared to trust fully, like Cedric, he was extremely wary of those outside his range.

'Just a minute,' said Cedric. 'Don't want to spill.'

He put the glasses down, reverently almost, and looked back at his trail; the carpet was still dry. Then he drew himself towards the formality of Attention as he faced his questioner.

'Well. What can I do for you, s——?' The word all but slid out. 'Sir.' They were officer material all right, this lot. But he could handle them. Ginger-head had caught the unpursued sibilant and attached it to the flights of speech he had heard before.

'In the Army were you?'

'Yes . . . Yes.'

'Regiment?'

'The Borders.'

'Good man. What made you get out?'

'Completion of twenty-five years service——' Yet again the sir rammed itself against his teeth. He drew himself up more stiffly.

'Twenty-five years, eh? Never 've thought it with all that—what-d'ye-me-call-it?—ton-up gear you're wearing. Hell's Angels stuff.'

Cedric glanced around at Josh in some panic. The jacket, the boots, all that he had made himself was being questioned and he had no defence. The girl laughed—but gently, sympathetic to Cedric's plight.

'What're you doing with yourself nowadays then, eh? I expect they gave you a good pension.'

'Jamie!' The girl tried to keep her tone light. 'You ask too many questions. And not even the right one. We wanted to know, if you'd be so kind,' she continued, determinedly talking over Jamie's riposte, 'if you'd any idea where we might find a cheap pub around here. The barman pretends there aren't any but I'm sure there must be. To stay the night,' she elaborated, as sweetness to the salt, 'somewhere nice and cheap.'

'As long as it's cheap,' said her other friend, 'it doesn't matter about the decor.'

'Let's see now, yes.' Cedric paused, considering; as if he knew. 'They *are* closed, mostly, in wintertime, for beds. But let's see . . .'

'There's plenty of places in Keswick,' said Josh abruptly, clutching at half-remembered hearsay to help his friend, staring at his feet as he spoke and digging his heels into the carpet. 'There's plenty there.' He stood up and looked at Cedric. 'Time we were away, eh?'

'Do have a drink,' said Jamie. 'Not often we get a chance to talk to you people who really live in this part of the world. Beautiful part of the world.' Cedric was undoubtedly flattered. '*Do* have a drink.'

'I'll wait outside then,' said Josh and he went towards the door, remembering the coat. Cedric's eyes followed him all the way and he turned back to the others, ashamed.

'He's very shy,' he said.

'You stay then. He said he'd wait.'

'I wouldn't enjoy it,' he replied, truthful in the detached state momentarily on him.

'Keswick,' said the girl. 'Thank you.'

'For God's sake, Ellen, we knew *that* for ourselves.'

Conscientiously, Cedric finished his Guinness. He grinned awkwardly and hesitated for a moment.

'Dis-*missed*!' ordered Jamie, hugely amused.

Cedric shuddered slightly and left.

Outside, Josh was sitting on the motor-bike, hands once more in his pockets, his breath appearing to pant out before his face. It was no longer snowing but there had been enough to cover the land and everywhere was black on white with the moonlight silvering the fronts of the fells.

'I'm sorry if I let you down,' said Josh, 'but I couldn't stick them.'

The apology and the confession so moved Cedric that his own repressed fury rushed up.

'They were effing sods! All of them. And that *Jamie*, bleeding *Jamie*! I've seen his type. I've dealt with his type before, see? You've got to be careful—you've got to play them along. That's what I was doing; you saw that? Heh? They think they can get away with anything. I—ignore them! Ball-less wonders!'

Cedric could not satisfy himself with words. He pulled out a small knife with a very ornate handle 'Watch,' he said.

He went over to a Land-Rover and peered inside it. Then, satisfied as to the ownership, he glanced around, bent down and jabbed the knife into the front tyre, stabbing it, several times. He moved to the back wheel.

'One's enough,' Josh called, softly. 'They'll have a spare for that.'

'No—the bloody lot, Josh old son—I'll get the bloody lot, me. They can't talk me down, spoil the evening, make me say "sir".'

'Just one.' Josh was firm. 'Maybe you shouldn't even have done that.'

Cedric held the knife poised dramatically, looking defiantly at Josh. The pub door opened and the beam of yellow light pointed at the Land-Rover. Cedric crouched down until the door was closed and was tense until the sound of the man's footsteps diminished.

'Right,' said Josh. 'Come on.'

Cedric jabbed at the tyre rather petulantly and unsuccessfully and then ran across towards Josh.

'Let's go!' Continuing the self-conceived drama, he kicked the starter urgently and roared away, without another word until they were well on from the place, half-way back to Ullaby.

On a small hill, he stopped and turned off the engine.

'What'll we do now then?'

'Why don't we go back,' said Josh, 'and go up top of Thorner's Hill?' This was a hillock just above the village and a path led down from it into the centre of the place.

'Why?'

'Just let's.' Josh grinned. 'Go on. I did what *you* wanted. Now it's your turn.'

Cedric, who had prepared himself for more bitterness and invective against those he now saw as his tormentors, was disarmed.

'All right. But there's no beer on Thorner's Hill.'

'Don't go by the village,' said Josh, 'use Pattinson's Lane.'

'All right.'

When they arrived where Josh had requested, the younger man jumped off the bike and immediately began packing together a large snowball. When he had made it hard and about as large as a football, he dropped it into the snow and pushed it along. It gathered more snow around it.

'I thought so.' Josh was pleased. 'It's that sticking kind of snow. We can have a monster snowball in no time.'

'Well, you great daft bugger,' said Cedric. 'Is that why you dragged me up this spot—risking my machine—just to make snowballs? Bloody hell's fire.' But he was pleased: he could not understand why this warmth and this pleasure spread into him.

'We could roll it down right into the street,' said Josh. 'I've worked out a road in my head. Just think of what they'll all say when they see it tomorrow morning!'

'If we rolled it near Calthwaite's cottage it would flood him out when it melted,' Cedric suggested.

'It's got to be near The Barn.' Spoken of thus, The Barn meant only one barn—that which had previously been a church. 'Think of the look on the kids' faces tomorrow morning.'

'What the hell for? Eh? This was your night off.'

'We could make a head for it even,' said Josh.

Absorbed, now, he ran the snowball backwards and forwards around the brow of the hill until it was above knee height.

'Come on, Cedric.'

The older man went across to help, soon giving orders as to how it should be steered, where packed tighter, changing Josh's route, ordering rests and calling for new efforts, less and less conscious of what he had thought of as the absurdity of it all as the white thing grew at their hands and the size of it made them laugh with excitement; for no reason, thought Cedric, for no reason—but that was what made Josh such a fantastic mate!—doing stupid things like this and being so happy about it, rolling this effing stupid snowball down Thorner's Hill, big enough to roll over the place itself and gather it up and send it down on to the plain and into the sea.

CHAPTER FOUR

MAUREEN fell for him as soon as he walked into the dance. She must have seen him around the place before but she had never noticed him, she would say, never *really* seen him until that Saturday night in Thurston Market Hall when he walked in wearing his black suit and his shirt undone (he could never bear a tie), so blond and so good-looking! She was sure she would have to join a queue! She thanked the Blessed Virgin she had no boyfriend at the time.

Maureen Telford was a Catholic, or rather she had been one. She was sure she was excommunicated now, never having been to Mass since she left school—the Catholic school in Thurston where all the teachers were priests and nuns and she recited and crossed daily in front of fine-looking hand-painted images. Maureen was almost eighteen, one of six children whose father was only occasionally employed and even when he was made not much more money than he could pick up from the Welfare State and the rivers all in his own time. He was well-noted for his fishing and his drinking and once he'd been a good fighter. She was dark-haired—but not as black as her sisters. She had let it grow long, and accentuated the length by a large hair-piece which was new that Saturday and had taken almost an hour to fix. It reared high her hair and made stately its settlement on her shoulders; her rather pale, slim face and the vivid use of mascara, lipstick and a shading which emphasized the cheekbones added to the wrought and dignified nature of the head. She was quite tall, her bust was not large, her legs were lean, thighs and hips slender, and the effect from neck to ankle was slight; so skimped were the clinging blouse and mini-skirt, so clean-lined and simple as to be a direct counter-statement to the luxuriant promises of the head.

They were thought of as a wild lot, the Telfords, the boys often in trouble, the mother and the girls as often near it, and while Maureen was a little apprehensive of this reputation there were times when she was glad of it, as now, for in the rough Saturday-night dance she could move across to stand with her family and so be protected from the drunks and the lunges of ignorant or frustrated men. She watched Josh from the moment he came in, never took her eyes off him and refused all dances except with her friend, Janet, who worked with her in the shop, and was overweight and not attractive.

Josh never danced and she was pleased, so very pleased that if she had still been a real Catholic she would have said a dozen Hail Marys straight off. He was so good-looking! Nobody else was as blond as he was! Usually people with blond hair had thin hair, but his was so thick! She noticed an oldish-looking man standing next to him, making a great thing of a half bottle of rum he had, but Josh did not drink any. And there was another man, Norman, she remembered his name, he went to all the dances and asked anybody and everybody to dance and away he would go spinning like a top until you told him to behave himself and then he'd try to do 'real, up-to-date' dancing but he'd put too much into it somehow and look stupid. He was funny with his grey hair and the way he laughed all the time and grinned. *She* had never danced with him although he had asked her more than once at different dances around the district. But now she found out that he worked with Josh and decided she would accept if he asked her this night and put herself out to catch his eye. He went back over to Josh and that other, black-haired oldish man who talked all the time to the Ullaby lot. They gathered, dance after dance, in a huddle like all the other village gangs: you could point them out along the walls—Oulton, Caldbeck, Kirkbride, Waverbridge, Fletchertown, Abbeytown, Bolton-Low-Houses, Ullaby. It was a good job none of the other towns had come to Thurston, that Aspatria and Silloth and Maryport had kept away. There was always trouble when they came—but tonight there needn't be a big fight though there would inevitably be some disturbance. Maureen had seen more fights in her own kitchen than most people see in a lifetime. Josh would have to be able to fight. He looked big enough, anyway.

She thought there might be some trouble when she saw Blister go over to Josh and push him on the shoulder in that menacingly friendly way. Blister lived on the same estate as Maureen and his family was always classed with hers and one or two others as the trouble-makers or the layabouts or whatever: she was a little afraid of him. She was worried that Josh might be frightened of Blister; and perhaps just as worried that he might take him on and be beaten—because Blister could really fight, fists, head, feet, knees, bottles, chairs, bricks, anything there was. Maybe Alex, her oldest brother, could match him: but no one else. And Alex and he usually fought on the same side against some gang from another place. It was terrible, in one way, how they just decided to get people and sometimes she hated them for it—but she would never miss a fight even though the sight of blood made her feel dizzy. Beth, her sister, who was here this night with her new husband Jack, had to be held back from joining in the kicking herself if she was drunk, which she often was on Saturday nights with her Bloody Marys. Maureen drank Babycham.

Blister had come in just after half-past ten. It was a wonder they let him in when he was so obviously plastered; there was a policeman at the door and the three bouncers, they could have banned him and it wouldn't have been the first time —he would have accepted it just as he was barred from most of the pubs in Thurston. It was only really The Lion and Lamb which properly tolerated him and that was because the landlord, Bobby Ismay, stood no nonsense from anybody and was known for it; besides, Molly, his wife was such a good-humoured woman you'd have to be very clever to upset her.

But Maureen was not really satisfied when Blister moved on. She had seen the Ullaby lot spread out when Blister and his brother had gone up to them, she had seen the tension in the movement of that black-haired man with the rum bottle (he had ended up by offering Blister a drink from the bottle: she knew he would do that, sucking up, his type were all like that!), she had seen Norman sidle away and keep a safe distance, she had felt the quiet rippling from the dropping of Blister into Josh's calm. But nothing happened. Blister had moved on, no display of contempt, just moved on.

There was a slow number and she managed to catch Norman's eye and over he bounded as if he'd been a yo-yo and the string on her finger.

Slow numbers meant you could talk. About half those at the dance slumped together in pairs, motionless to the uncultured eye; of the rest, most chatted and girded themselves for the final push before 11.15 p.m. when the dance would end so as not to run over into the Sabbath and make it unholy. Norman held Maureen at arm's length: he fancied her but feared her brothers more and would not presume.

Now that she had the opportunity to ask about Josh (she desperately wanted to know if he already had a girlfriend and was not dancing tonight because she was not here and he was being faithful; she found herself almost praying this might be so), she could find no words. Yet she must, for otherwise Norman would assume that she had wanted to dance with him for himself alone. He was daft enough to—they were strange, these farm people, forever grinning at you and hoisting you about like a sack of potatoes: she made no attempt to follow him, just made sure he did not step on her new patent shoes with the large gold buckles and tried to keep Josh in sight. He was so lovely! She was rather startled that she could even think that, she would never have said it in public under any but the most abnormal circumstances and even to say it to herself seemed a bit soft . . . But he *was*. She wanted to feel his soft cheek against hers, just rubbing against hers.

'Penny for your thoughts,' said Norman: it was an opening which rarely failed, he had discovered.

'That all?'

'A tanner.'

'The last of the big spenders.'

'Who's your friend was dancing with you?'

'You know her.'

'I don't.'

'I'm often with her.'

'It's her *name* I don't know,' Norman explained, patiently.

'What do you want her name for?'

'What d'ye think?'

'Fancy her, then?' And Maureen was dismayed that she was a little jealous; how stupid!

'No. I just want to know what to call her.'

'Call her for what?'

'You're so sharp you'll cut yourself. She's a bit fat, anyway.'

'You're no matchstick.'

'I'm not a woman.'

'Three guesses.'

'Alice?'

'No.'

'Mary?'

'No . . . What made you say Alice? Why did you think of Alice?'

'I don't know.'

'There must be *some* reason.'

'Mrs Wilson's called Alice.'

'Who's Mrs Wilson?'

'Where I'm hired. My boss's missis.'

'Where you're hired with, with—that—Josh isn't it?'

'Aha! Swop you.'

'Janet.'

'Josh Lawton. Janet who?'

'Sands. Why doesn't he dance?'

'He never does. He's very shy.'

'He doesn't seem shy,' she lied, to keep it going, 'at least, he seems to keep acting the goat with that black-haired fella with the rum bottle.'

'Cedric. Cedric Tyson.'

'Where does he come in?'

'He's been in the Army for a long time. Just comes back on leave and either stays in Ullaby or goes for long rides on a motor-bike. He's out for good now.'

'You don't seem to like him anyway.'

'Least said,' Norman replied, primly.

'He's quite attractive in his own way,' Maureen persisted. 'Dark . . . mysterious-looking . . . he looks . . . experienced. I suppose that's the Army.'

'My lips are sealed . . .' said Norman.

Maureen was cross: unable to resist teasing Norman, she'd steered away from her subject. But there was one point which could, validly, bring her back to it, she decided after she had endured Norman's shuffles in silence for a few moments.

'Was Blister looking for a fight?' she asked.

'Well, I don't think he was searching for buried treasure.'

'Who's the clever socks now?'

The dismissive tone of her reply rather dashed Norman. He was already conscious that he had not been beckoned over for the pleasure of his company but was disheartened to discover that his company gave so little. And that particular rejoinder of his about buried treasure was one he'd used hundreds of times without any trouble at all: often it had raised a smile. Maureen felt his interest running away from her but knew that her own authority in the matter of fights would compel his attention and was content enough with that: she was tired of his interest.

'He looked to me as if he came in wanting to fight the first fella he saw.'

'He did say something about it,' Norman was sulky. He was merely being used as a way to latch on to Josh; though not entirely unaccustomed to such a role he still felt sore.

'What exactly?'

'Said something about Josh's training.'

'What training?'

'He trains for fell-racing. Cedric trains him. They go out almost every night. Blister saw them, he said, when he was up there after some rabbits.'

'What exactly did he say?'

'I can't remember.'

'You can but you won't say. What did *Josh* say?'

'He just laughed.'

'And Blister let him?'

'He always just laughs. You'll never see Josh get in trouble. There's no bad in the man.' Norman expanded a little, almost paternally, warmed by the necessity, as he saw it, to explain and defend the good reputation of his friend. 'He could be sat in a thieves' kitchen, Josh, and it wouldn't come to blows.'

'He wouldn't be sat long in our kitchen without one or two.'

'There's no harm in him, you see,' Norman was soon made sentimental. 'Bad goes to bad. Good to good.'

'That Cedric doesn't look much good to me.'

Norman frowned and did not reply. They were quite near Josh and Cedric and he looked at the grinning ex-soldier with his arm around Josh's shoulder, hauling the lad's ear to his mouth to whisper some irrelevant intimacy, no doubt—acting as if he *owned* the boy and Josh not seeming to *mind*! Then he glanced at Maureen.

'Come and meet him.'

'Oh no.'

'Come *on*.' He pretended to drag her and she pretended to resist a little. 'Come on—it's what you've been wanting all the time.'

'Don't shout!' she said, truly disconcerted: and then, once more pretending, 'You're hurting my arm.'

Norman parted Josh and Cedric.

'Josh, this is Maureen. She wants to dance with you but she's over-shy to ask herself. Go on, man, get hold of her.'

It was partly the surprise of it which took Josh into her arms and into the dance—a fate he would generally avoid at almost any cost; but also it was her beauty which moved him. He was to say, 'I'd only to see her for a second and that was it.'

Maureen later reported that it was like walking around with a tree-trunk. 'He was that wooden I expected him to come out in leaves.' They exchanged no word and kept the distance they had found or rather fallen into in that first clumsy clutch. Maureen did look at Josh once but the poor man's face was so full of confusion that she spared him any more and kept her eyes firmly on his shoulder, only occasionally catching the glances of Janet (nodding to her with a rocking motion as if her heels were stuck in rubber balls) and Beth, who mimed being both (coarsely) pleased and impressed. There was no doubt that it was something to get him to dance with you at all.

When they suddenly switched to a fast number, Maureen let herself go for a minute or two and Josh just stood there, fists clenched, arms and body stiff, face strained, gamely but helplessly shifting from foot to foot and looking longingly at the walls as to a refuge. She took pity and led him there. She was sure, she said later, that if she had just walked off he would have said nothing and when challenged with this he would laugh in such a way that you could not tell. But she stayed and they danced once more together, having painfully exchanged commonplaces, brief between the lengths of silence. And in the last dance she felt him relax a little and took the hint, pressed herself against him and was both mischievously and tenderly pleased to hear his sigh of surprise and pleasure.

He did not ask to see her home and she had taken the initiative often enough for one night, she thought. 'See you again,' was all she said, but he had instantly replied, 'Yes,' and almost added 'Please'.

Cedric's motor-bike was not there and Josh assumed he must have gone on alone. He was surprised; it was unlike the man to leave him like that. The arrangement was always that he would give him a lift back after a dance. Norman came on his bicycle and a cross-bar would have been handy enough but Norman had been seen chatting away to Janet and would probably be seeing her home.

How they could talk, Cedric and Norman, just chatter away to anybody no matter who, always find something to say. He'd been like a mute with Maureen, he knew, and was tormented in his mind by awareness of that, but what was there to say? What *did* they say, the others? He liked to listen to her; there need be nothing said; just to look was enough and hold her.

He decided to walk back along a by-road which led past Old Carlisle, site of a Roman camp. He remembered a few such facts about the immediate neighbourhood—things like that seemed to Josh to bring it honour which gave him great satisfaction. He went along the Syke Road and then turned into the way which would lead him past the camp and on the few miles to Ullaby. The moon was bright, there was no wind: he could spend all the time, every step, nursing the image of Maureen.

Maureen scarcely realized why she had stayed up so late. Everyone had gone to bed except herself and Beth who slept in the sitting room with her husband on a put-you-up which by day was a leatherette settee; they had their names down for a council house but the list was long. When the sisters were alone, however, she understood that she had wanted to have something confirmed and, as they were tired and not much given to oblique or circumlocutory ways, she asked straight out: 'What d'you think of him?'

'Your Josh?'—Beth, who had taken off her blouse in front of the mirror to see her own breasts it seemed, for there was no other reason—'Well,' she questioned her image which was considering its reflection rather critically, 'he's good-looking all right but I don't think he'd do much for me. Something soft about him.'

'What d'you mean, soft?' Maureen was angry; remembering that she had thought, and still in some crevice of her mind did think, that Josh had side-stepped that challenge from Blister. He ought to have taken it up: her brothers would have done.

'I don't know. Why won't my bloody hair stay wavy for more than a night at a stretch? What stuff do *you* use?'

'Stay-Silk. What's soft about him?'

'He just seems it, that's all. I mean—he, you know, what is it?—blushes, that's what I mean. You'd think he was back at school.'

Maureen blushed. Her sister bounced her breasts. 'Nothing sagging about that lot, eh? Bloody Sylvia Carruthers said that women's tits started to sag from the day they were married. Silly old tart.'

Maureen turned away from her sister. She had felt the tears lurch on to the bottom lids and though as a family they cried freely among themselves, each hated to be the one to begin it.

'You're crying.'

'I am not.'

'You *are*!' That established, Beth, too, felt her lips quiver. 'Oh, baby, I'm sorry. You've *fallen* for him, haven't you?' She came round the table and sat next to her youngest sister, 'And he's so lovely and all I do is make fun of him.'

'Well,' Maureen was not yet sobbing though the tears were

running steadily, 'he's *not* soft.'

'Of course he's not. He's great . . . Everybody knows Josh is OK. Do you love him?'

'Oh Beth! How can you ask that?'

And now Maureen did sob, loudly and emphatically.

'You do, don't you? You *do*.' Somehow Beth could not cry: her moment had passed or it had not arrived; she even felt awkward touching the hunched shoulders of her sister and was a little irritated at being excluded from such a good feeling as love and such a deep satisfaction as tears.

'There's no need to cry,' she said, almost sharply. 'He's obviously crackers about you so you're all right.'

Inadvertently, perhaps, she had said the one thing Maureen had wanted to hear and the girl turned and looked her straight in the face, the expression of love and hope, tremulous with tears and excitement, making Beth wince with something like envious nostalgia.

'Is he? Oh, do you really think he likes me? Really? Oh, Beth! I think I'm in love with him.'

It was a night when nothing that moved outdoors seemed to want to sleep. Even the grass and the hedges seemed to stretch with pleasure, reaching for the moon as if it were the sun. The fells were hugely black and gentle before him, ravines of shadow and slopes of pale yellow. In this true sea of calm, Ullaby was like a ship anchored on the breast of a wave, the fell undulating about it, and the slate roofs like sails there, shining in the moonlight.

The vicar was leaning on the gate to the path which led over the last field to the village. It was as if he had been waiting for Josh, so easily did he meet his approach. The disruption caused by their separation had long since been fogotten and now there was an affectionate friendship between the labourer and the retired clergyman whom the younger man always referred to, most earnestly, as 'the best man ever was'. Josh was whistling. He stopped abruptly when he saw the vicar.

'Good evening.'

'Hello, Joshua. It's morning, I think: yes, half-past the hour —the Lord's Day once more.'

'A good start to it anyway. You couldn't have a better night than this.'

'No, indeed. And you can feel all of nature enjoying it, can't you? Turning over in her sleep like the huge goddess she is, and across her limbs scurry the night creatures and on her brow is the dew. The Greeks were right about all that. It's so sweet this peace this time of night, Joshua, and yet I want to fill it with talk, I always do, you know. I stayed at Fellways for company, you know, because I thought "there will always be boys and boys will always chatter". I could have moved elsewhere . . . But what you hide from will find you out . . . What are *you* most afraid of, Joshua?'

'I don't know, sir. Nothing that I can think of . . . there's bound to be something, though.'

'You're so obliging you must be modest even about your courage. I never met a boy so frank as you. And in the dark, even in the moonlight, I can detect that blush. Let me tell you, Josh—you're afraid of being asked to speak out in front of others.'

'Yes. I am. That's true.'

'And so eager to confirm it! Well—you see—perhaps one day you'll have to stand in front of the entire public, all your friends, Josh, all Ullaby, maybe even all of Thurston as well, and speak out! There. Don't shake your head. I just tease you to keep you here when you'll be wanting to be in bed. Sundays: work for you, too, isn't it? Shepherds and pastors, priests and farmers, how often have they been yoked together in poetry and song. I won't keep you.'

'Will *you* be . . . ?' There was something so tentative about the young man's enquiry; it sprang from the same source of innocence which the vicar had always thought a wonder and marvelled how it kept in bounds.

'I'll be fine. I've at least four pipes of tobacco and I can be in Thurston in an hour and a half. I don't mind the walk as long as I know I'm going somewhere. And Sergeant Howard's on duty tonight—he's an excellent man, most understanding and full of stories. Especially after a Saturday night. I hope you don't feature in any of them, Joshua, but I don't really have to fear that. I know.'

'Good night then.'

He opened the gate to let the boy pass and to ease his going, and himself set out for Thurston, sacrificing a great deal by not imposing more on his former pupil which he could well have done and easily, for Josh was unhappy at the thought of his old protector's unhappiness and would have passed an hour with him gladly.

But how much better on his own! On that wet path of ripe night smells. With Maureen; still hot on his palms the feeling of her back, still fresh on his lips the crush of her hair, and her face blazing in his mind illuminated by this first love.

CHAPTER FIVE

CEDRIC had watched them dancing together. He had signalled to Josh but the younger man had scarcely acknowledged him and Cedric had not wanted to make his curiosity conspicuous.

He had discovered her name and the information added a further measure of caution; it would be foolish to do anything to upset *that* family.

'I hope he knows what he's handlin',' he said to Norman, speaking out of the corner of his mouth. 'I mean we all know where she comes from and who she belongs to and that's trouble.' His worry was momentarily directed to this possibility. 'We won't be able to take them on,' he said, with some pride in the unassailability of the force hypothetically ranged against him. 'If it looks like breaking—move, that's all we can do—move on.'

'It seems to me she wants more of a cuddle than a scrap,' Norman replied. 'If you don't think about fights they don't come.'

'You just wait till the end of this dance.'

But Josh went to another part of the hall with Maureen and Cedric shook Norman's shoulder.

'What the rotten hell did you push that tart on to him for, anyway?'

'Excuse me,' said Norman, coolly taking pleasure in Cedric's increasing concern. 'I think I'll have a dance myself.' He went over to Janet.

Others from Ullaby drifted away, in the quest to scrounge a promise of the last dance from someone. Cedric sucked on his rum bottle—his regular weekly treat—and moved back towards the wall as the floor filled up with slow-moving couples, clutching each other tightly. Josh passed quite close to him without even seeing him; and at that Cedric left the place.

'He can effing walk back,' he said to himself.

He rode to Ullaby. If Josh preferred the effing company of bleeding others—sod him! That was fine—no hard feelings. He speeded up when he came into the village.

He was sweating. The air was mild and the army coat which he had put on as a windbreaker seemed to have brought on this heavy sweat. He sluiced himself down in the back kitchen—opening his shirt front, splashing water under his armpits, doing the thing properly.

The frying-pan was deep in grease. He looked at it as he was drying himself, then suddenly picked it up and banged and banged it on the cooker. Effing filthy soddin' bloody rotten stupid *muck*! Who the hell for Christ's sake can eat from that and not be sick as a rotten pig? Damn! Damn! Damn! Damn! Damn!

He stopped and listened for his mother upstairs. But she would not come unless called: stood at the door of her bedroom, sullenly waiting for his mood to pass. Cedric took the long handle of the frying-pan and bent it double: then he threw it at the wall.

He buttoned up his shirt rapidly.

'I can't let him walk back. He'll be exhausted for tomorrow, to train. Anyway, must do the decent thing.' That's what one of his officers had never stopped saying. 'Must do the decent thing.'

In some part of his mind he had worked out that if Josh had taken Maureen home he would be through with it by now and setting out on his way back. He decided against his greatcoat and ran upstairs for his leather jacket. The house shook.

'To bed with you, to bed with you, you old spy eh?' He was in fine spirits. His mother opened her door and watched him.

'Good night.' He grinned fiercely at her as he rushed down the stairs. 'WOWOWO WOWOWOWO!!' The exhilaration he felt was too painful to be contained. He jumped the last three stairs and once more the small cottage trembled.

He missed Josh and drove around between Thurston and Ullaby for about three hours, telling himself continuously how calm he was and how nice a night it was for such a ride. All the time he kept his headlight full on, refusing to dip it for any oncoming cars as one refusing to bow the knee and submit —this was how he saw it.

The vicar, too, he missed, for the old man took a path of his own down to the plain, preferring to cross the fields from farm to farm, at each awakening a dog so that he was bayed down from the fells, his torch a faint speck of unnecessary light on the moon-shadowed land.

As he mowed his way back and forth, Cedric's feeling intensified without any clarification. He had no way of describing them to himself, no way that he could accept.

He stopped in Thurston when he saw the vicar coming up Market Hill, and the clergyman motioned on the policeman with whom he had been walking.

'I'll be with you in a moment, officer.' As one who also loved Josh, the vicar instantly guessed at Cedric's condition.

'He's back home.' He gave the answer without the question being asked and Cedric did not notice the omission, only felt the presence of a concern similar to his own. He could talk now.

'It was just that I wanted to make sure he was all right.'

'Of course.'

'This, er, this tart, this girl you see—her family—they're a rough lot and I wanted to make sure he was all right. He *was* all right when you saw him, wasn't he?'

'Yes. Perfectly.'

'That's good then. Hm! *You* know old Josh—you have to watch out for him sometimes—he doesn't seem to recognize things that are good for him and things that aren't. It's funny really. Anyway—when was it you saw him?'

'About—oh, it must have been three hours ago. It's almost four o'clock, you know.'

'Yes. Well. As long as he was all right. Good then. Right.' He made no attempt to move.

'Good night then,' the vicar spoke gently and released him.

Cedric did not reply but let off the brake and rolled silently down the hill. The old man watched him go. 'You are right,' he said, 'someone must look after Josh.'

The engine ignited and the motor-bike tore up the silence of the town as it fled back towards the fells.

Cedric spent most of the next day in his bedroom. He saw Josh biking down towards Thurston at midday and calculated that he must have missed his dinner to be so early. He felt sick in his stomach and could not follow him.

He did not get changed all day but lay on his bed in the gaudy silk dressing-gown he had once so keenly delighted to wear.

As soon as he had finished his morning's work on the farm, Josh took out his bicycle and prepared to set off for Thurston. He could not bear to wait the hour for his dinner, so from the attic he collected some apples and Mrs Wilson disapprovingly cut into her Sunday chocolate cake to give him a slice. He would not listen to her scolding about the dangers which would result from skipping so well and long prepared a meal (shepherd's pie, his favourite) nor would he tell her where he was going (though she quickly guessed from the stammerings and the silences) and so he left her rather sulky, but he was too full of Maureen to see or care. He did not even change: kept on the short wellingtons, the jeans that were stuffed into them, the shirt made from material similar to the jeans, an old neck-scarf, a battered jacket and on the back of his head, a cap. Tall and lean, he looked both hickish and yet somehow dashing, country cousin and yet, as he ran with the bike and vaulted on to the seat, somehow also cavalryman.

'You can't go like that!' Norman shouted because he was scandalized. He had no need to raise his voice for Josh was circling around him in the farmyard, eating the chocolate cake in the security of that sheltered square. 'Not on a Sunday, you can't go like that! She'll have a fit—I don't care who she is—no real *lady* can go mad on a man in wellingtons.'

Josh crammed the chocolate cake into his mouth with both hands, the bike wobbled and made for a quiet cluster of hens which scattered wildly.

'Put some shoes on at least. And that cap! They don't fancy caps nowadays, Josh—they're too old-fashioned. Use your own hair and leave it at that.'

'Not taking her out,' Josh spoke through a wad of cake. 'Just going to look at her. Not going out with her.'

'You mean you didn't make a date?'

'No.' Josh grinned, held up both sticky hands and then licked his fingers as he continued to swirl around Norman, standing there turning with a bucket of feed in each hand.

'You're slower than a skinflint's treat,' said the older man with relish; it was another of his special phrases. 'Are you going all the way to Thurston and back on that boneshaker just on the off-chance of getting a quick look at her then?'

'YES. I AM! I AM! YAM! YAM! YAM!'

And Josh raced for the gate, along the track and away down from the hills on to the plain, the apples in his jacket pockets lifting it out behind him like wings as he put the bike in top gear and pedalled where he could have free-wheeled, swooping down on the closed-up Sunday town this grey spring morning, his eyes streaming against the wind.

It was Janet who rescued him from his hungry and fruitless circuits of the housing estate. He was cold; the day had turned back to winter; his hands and face were bluish. Janet came down the pathway from her house, face crowned by a cluster of curlers, pink fluffy slippers flapping, arms folded tightly, hugging herself. She smiled teasingly.

'Looking for Maureen?'

'Eh?'

Josh had been leaning against a lamp-post; still on the bike, both himself and the machine propped against the lamp-post.

'Maureen?'

'. . . Just biking around.'

'She lives at 46 Derwent Avenue. She should be in unless they've gone out in Jackie's car for a run. Jackie's her brother-in-law . . . don't look so worried.'

He had not been looking worried, just a shiver of cold, but Janet knew how these things worked out and she was not going to have her pattern disturbed. 'You'll be all right,' she reassured him, heavily. 'I could tell she fancied you.'

Josh gripped the handlebars and prepared to leave: there was something unbearably intrusive about this entry into his private world and yet he could not just push off without hurting her feelings. She never took her eyes off him.

'Should I go and get her for you?'

'No.'

'Why not? What're you doing here if you don't want me to get her? You're just shy, aren't you? I'll get her.' She smiled happily as if she had made the match. 'I can tell you're shy.'

She turned and shuffled away in her slippers, still hugging herself, and Josh was powerless to stop her: nor could he leave, as he so much wanted to, for Maureen would hear of it and be offended.

'Janet!' he called out. 'Janet. It's all right. I'm . . . I'm—not dressed up enough to talk to her.'

Janet glanced over her black-sweatered shoulder and the silver curlers nodded in cheerful certainty. 'She won't mind. Don't *worry*. And don't be so *shy*.' The last remark, based on original observation, pleased her more than any other and she beamed plumply and happily at Josh, who had no defence against such relentless kind concern. 'I'll give you a lift on my crossbar then.

The alternative was to follow her slow pad at her slow pace and that would mean more talking; enough had been said, in every possible sense. Janet sank deeply on to the cold cross-bar and stuck her feet out stiffly before her.

At Maureen's she trotted up the garden path and round to the back door to reappear through the front door almost like a conjurer with an impeccably dressed Maureen pulling on mauve gloves.

'She was on her way out anyway!' Janet shouted. 'Another two minutes and you'd have missed her.'

Maureen had glanced at him and then glanced away again and Josh wished with every corpuscle that he were far away. But he was stuck. Janet appeared to conduct her friend down the path to the small green gate. She stood firm, once through it, seeing all, hearing all and prepared to say all, superintending this fragile encounter as a wardress might look over a prisoner and her visitor.

'Hello,' said Maureen, more to hold her own before her old friend than to greet her new one.

Josh had great difficulty but did reply, 'Hello.'

'You look cold,' said Maureen. 'Have you biked here?'

'I'm not cold.'

'Blue's just the colour of his skin!' Janet creased herself in mirth.

'I have to go to a christening,' said Maureen. 'I'm frightened to be late.' She hesitated: he was far too scruffy to come with her, but was he so bad that he could not even see her there?

'Well I'll be off then,' Josh replied: he made no move.

'It's Kathleen Haile's: do you know her?'

Josh shook his head.

'A boy. I'm a witness. That's what they call them in her church. She works with me.' Maureen glanced rather desperately at Janet still standing there arms folded: Maureen was pushed to talk more than she would have done just by Janet's presence. 'Well then.'

'I'll be away then,' said Josh and this time he did something; he edged the front wheel away from the kerb—concentrating fully on this action.

Maureen felt the eyes and ears of the estate, all the company of council tenants bearing witness to this meeting, and she was not going to be seen to be scared or at a loss.

But there was nothing she could say. It was Josh had to make the move. It was all very well for him to look like a dream; there were times when you have to talk as well; she could not do it for him.

Josh alternated between wanting to flee and a new sensation which took him unawares, wanting to stay forever, to marry her on the spot; he was so moved that she should stand there in the cold shivering and looking so beautiful, being dressed-up and talk to a dunce like himself. He wished it were the christening of their child she were going to.

'I could meet you after the christening,' he dared, abruptly. 'I could be changed by then.'

'You could go the Carlisle pictures,' said Janet.

'That would be great.' Maureen smiled at him, as if blessing his initiative.

'Meet you on—Market Hill then, at the bus-station, at about six o'clock.'

'There's a bus every hour and on the hour,' said Janet.

'Just before six then,' said Maureen.

'Yes!' Josh looked at her directly for the first time that afternoon, unblushing and without fears: the clarity of her returned look made straight for his feelings where it dissolved all the confusions of anxiety and hesitation and beamed on him the news of her love. As if an invisible God-sized hand had reached out and plucked him, he shoved away the bike, kicked the pedals into action, forced speed from the rattling machine and raced off. The devil could have been on his tail: on his face was the realization that he was in love; in love, in love, in love.

The next night he was waiting for Josh—away from the village, half-way to Thurston, in a side-lane, sitting on his motor-bike. He had skipped his tea and come straight down from the quarry. Josh flashed past him so quickly on his bicycle that Cedric was taken by surprise. Then he had trouble kicking the engine into life. When he did turn on the road, Josh was out of sight. He opened up the throttle.

In the spring evening, with the hills still bare and emptiness around, Josh heard the sound of Cedric's bike and, beaming to himself, pedalled faster, slinging himself low around corners on this old racing-bike, shooting down to Thurston. The nearer Cedric came, and the more furiously he pedalled and when his friend came beside him he pretended not to notice but laughed to himself and raced his machine against the motor-bike.

Cedric went ahead and stopped across the road. Josh flew at him and then braked, over-hard, and skidded into the verge and into the ditch. He took his time about coming back on to the road. Cedric held himself back from speech only by making the greatest effort and when the words did come out they carried the sting and sulk of enforced suppression.

'What about your training? What about our schedule? What about that? I'm just asking. There's no need to answer. I couldn't care less what you do. Your life's your own. But we had a bloody schedule. I was training you. I don't mind—just say it's all over—say it—OK—that's fine. That's effing bloody marvellous after all the rotten work we've put into it, that's typical. Not a word he says to me—not one rotten effing word

—I turn up and he's not there. Nothing. I don't mind. Take my word for *that*. There's plenty I can do without training you every bloody night of the week. But you're throwing it away. Remember that. We had a plan and you're throwing it all away. I'm saying nothing but you'll regret it. You'll turn one of these days and you'll regret it. And it'll be too late. That schedule I've worked out takes you right up to it—mess about with it and you need never have started. I've worked that out from all over the place. *Throw* it in my face—go on! Tell me you're sick of it all. Go on! Just say! That's all—just—tell—me —straight—out!'

Cedric had never spoken to him in that tone before. He had often harangued him about training and about mannerisms he disapproved of, but never in this way.

'I'm going down to see Maureen,' Josh replied. 'That's all.'

'That's enough. Right!' Cedric kicked the motor-bike. 'That's all you needed to say. Right!' He revved up, and hidden in the noise was his scream which he dared not let out unprotected: then he lessened the volume of it. 'It's all off, then, our—partnership—say no *more*—it's something you do properly or not at all—fine; good; great, in fact—great! Just when you were getting in some sort of bloody shape, you stupid git! Oh—shit! You've WASTED yourself!'

He opened up and the bike bucked off, almost knocking Josh over as it rampaged up the wrong side of the road and made for the hills as if intending to drive a tunnel through them.

CHAPTER SIX

ON the first really hot Sunday they took a bus and went to the beach at Silloth. Once in the seaside town they ignored the Promenade and the Green, the Entertainments and the Bandstand and walked over the railway lines and through the small docks to the West Beach. Here were dunes which hid a warrenful of lovers, sand nearer white than brown, grass which could cut your skin and the grey-blue sea beating up the flat Solway 'faster than a galloping horse'.

They took towels and bathing-costumes and Maureen made sandwiches and then there was a small difficulty, for she hated carrying bags about on such a free afternoon and yet what was the alternative? If you went to Silloth you had to swim—and Maureen was a good swimmer, quite eager to show off this skill to Josh, who had confessed that he could do not more than splash about. She tried to squeeze everything into a large handbag which had at least some semblance of style even though it was over a year out of date—a baggy purple pouch with tassels all along the edge—but the towels were too bulky. It had to be a carrier-bag and when Josh offered to carry it she was even more irritated. The feeling of irritation stayed with her on the crowded double-decker bus and it was not until they were on the cinder path which led away from the docks to the West Beach that she could bring herself into a good mood.

'I'm sorry I've been so snappy,' she said and moved close to him.

'That's all right.'

Whenever he looked down at her so relaxed and smiling she

wanted to reach up, put an arm around his neck and force a kiss on him. But she hesitated this time: something in his tone checked her.

'I mean, I haven't had a good word to say to you since we left the house.'

'That's all right.'

'You hadn't noticed!'

'Hm?'

'You just have not noticed, have you? You haven't taken any notice.'

'What of?'

'Me being snappy . . .'

'Just as well then, isn't it?' Once more he smiled at her.

'No.'

'Why not?'

She could find no reply but moved away, trying to discover words for her complaint but unable to.

At the first beach-hut refreshment place they bought a large bottle of lemonade with a corkscrew top. Then they went over the dunes and on to the deep sand. Maureen took her shoes off.

To their right was the old pier, jutting out forlornly, an unemphatic reminder to the maritime history of the place. To their left, sand, and the gentle curve of the coastline past Allonby down to Maryport. The beach was crowded near the refreshment chalets, and they walked away from the crowd, seeking a place of some privacy like other young couples.

Maureen was wearing the bottom part of her bikini and it was not much trouble to wriggle into the top bit. She did not wait for Josh but ran straight into the sea and swam out as if unconcerned about the coldness of the water or the swiftness of the outgoing tide. Josh dawdled out of his clothes and walked to the edge of the sea reluctantly. Maureen was far out by this time.

His skin was very white and the cool wind from the Firth made his flesh crimp: the elegant strength which marked him so strongly when he was dressed was masked by his embarassed nakedness.

He picked up some pebbles and played ducks and drakes.

Maureen had been too confident. When she turned she felt the force of the current and her throat thickened with fear. Only Josh was anywhere near, but even he would not hear if she called out to him. And he could not swim. She talked to herself: 'Just don't panic, don't panic.' The words made her feel even more strange.

She saw the ripple of the water relentlessly pushing towards her and she licked her lips to take off the salt. It was strange but her body felt dry: in that sea her flesh felt dry and without nerves or muscles or will. The prayers droned in some pit of her mind but mostly, in those few seconds, she was aware of the water streaming over the dry skin and Josh on the shore sending pebbles skimming across the surface of the waves. It was as if the sky became a still dome stretched to silence; and the distant crowds on the beach had no more presence than the long grasses swaying on the dunes; even Josh lost the power he had and stood there as a bloodless white figure. It was the pebbles she watched, bouncing on the top of the waves; and this heavy sea-water pushing into her feeble arms outstretched to meet it but prepared neither for an effort nor for an embrace.

As if despite herself, outside the knowledge of that frightened self which was nearly paralysed with panic and wonder, her arms began to pull at the water, her fingers bent, drawing it down as if her nails were tearing solid material. Even that small gesture made a difference. She pulled harder and once more she spoke 'Josh . . . Josh'—but his name had scarcely the strength to come through her lips. She kicked out her legs and fought against this current.

She only had to stay in the same place and the current would take the water past her. The thought that she had only to stay where she was, this sight of herself left in that spot on the beach after the tide had gone out gave her comfort and relieved her in some way, penetrated the fearful shell of stillness which had threatened her. She felt herself making progress.

The picture grew stronger; she saw herself suddenly landed on the beach by the desertion of the sea, lying there trailing seaweed and smudged by the wet sand. It inspired her to battle for herself.

She pulled steadily at the swift tide until she felt the sea-bed under her feet. She swam a little more to emphasize her victory and then stood up and trudged through the water towards Josh. She ought to walk right past him. He watched her nervously, ready to dodge should she kick up the water and splash him. She came up to him and stared into his face.

'Didn't you see me?'

'Yes.'

'Well.'

'Yes—you're a *really* good swimmer. I would sink in a puddle, me. Hey!'

Maureen had reached out and put her arms around him and he wriggled to be free of her clammy coldness. She shivered violently and pressed herself against him and then, to his embarrassment because it was a public place, she pulled his face down to her own and kissed it again and again.

Maureen went to Ullaby only once in those first few weeks which later were to be looked back on as the time when happiness moved ceaselessly through all feelings and actions: and on that showery Sunday afternoon she knew herself to be under scrutiny as never before. She enjoyed the experience. She clung to Josh as they walked through the village (he, walking a little too quickly for her, holding her arm a little too tightly and too high) and simulated shivers and did in fact blush, but she liked being there in her new black skirt and the very dark brown nylon tights with the new big-buckled patent shoes and a dark brown coat in a sort of washed leather (synthetic) material. She queened it in grey Ullaby where the only girls she saw were lumpy in their big brothers' sweaters and bought-to-last wellingtons, heaving themselves across farmyards with pails of fodder. The boys who passed up and down the road turned to pass again and yet again, and were bold each time with their yells ringing and the cheekier yells to Josh and whoops of pleasure in the legs and the face and the style—they were as flattering as any courtier, as much a compliment as any words. In that mood, the village looked to her a pretty little spot. They had climbed Thurston's hill to a seat which was newly inscribed:

and looked down on Thurston, easily picked out by the factory chimney and Highmoor Tower, and beyond it to the sea; it made you feel good, in some way, looking down on the place in which you had passed all your life, it made you feel you could do things. In Ullaby there would be no Beth and no drunk dad to be embarrassed by, no pestering from her brothers for money and their friends for favours, no being a Telford and expected to be tough and hard-faced, no more having to go home every night to the worst part of the estate where everybody knew they had put all the hard-case families, all the difficult ones who didn't keep their houses properly or neglected their gardens or made too much noise.

When she told Beth that she would not mind living in Ullaby, her sister was critical.

'You'll be lost in a week,' she said, 'in that hole. Who lives there? A few old farmers—and they're as tight as ticks, and then all the leftovers who didn't have the brains to get out—no offence to your fella; he's different. You'd hate it.'

'What's so special about the people in Thurston then? Same old faces just the same.'

'Ullaby's a hole. That's all, love; the end of the line. Go there, and you'll stay there and drop dead.'

'Thank *you*. You're just jealous because Josh could get us a cottage to live in right away.'

'Going with Old Muddy Boots has made you a bit of a bitch, love.'

'Don't call me "love". You only use it when you're sarcastic.'

'Diddums.'

'Bugger off.'

'Naughty. What would the old vicar say? Eh? What would your friend's old crackpot friend have to say about that? I've heard about him talking to you and Josh and giving you his blessing and that. Strikes me he's trailing round after you for the view . . .'

'You need your mind spring-cleaning—if you knew what a brush was for.'

'I know a brush, my love. I hope your Josh has as good an idea of a handle.'

'What's *that* supposed to mean?'

'Well. He *is* a bit slow, isn't he?'

'I'll slap your chops if you don't shut them.'

'Try it.'

'. . . I wouldn't dirty my hands.'

Maureen blew on her nails and then rubbed them on her blouse. They were immaculate. She worked in Studholme's clothes shop and though she was the most junior girl she still had to look smart at her job. Beth went down to the factory in much the same state as their mother went off to her seasonal potato-picking. It was a sore distinction. Beth took her time to let it work its way through her mind before replying: 'Stuck-up little twat.'

Which Maureen counted as something of a victory. 'I like that place,' was all she answered. Then added, 'I could live there,' out of bravado.

It was Wilson who had suggested the cottage to Josh—there was one available near the farm, a cottage traditionally inhabited by the married man among the hired labourers. There had always been one until recently when machinery had halved and then quartered Wilson's labour-force and the two men left were single—Norman and Josh. So the cottage had been empty for about five years, though, a careful man, Wilson had seen that it had not gone to ruin. Josh, unknowingly working for his own best ends, had been the one to keep it up; it was a comfortable place, a little isolated but near enough the village centre. It was Mrs Wilson who had suggested that Mr Wilson mention the cottage to Josh. They had no children of their own, this cautious Methodist pair, and the notion of a young family somehow attached to her, though at a satisfactory distance, appealed greatly to the farmer's wife. She declared, also, that she had quite taken to Maureen. She saw her only the once, on that brave parade through Ullaby—where Josh had certainly not introduced her to anyone, all his effort buckled to the labour of walking through the handful of houses without being paralysed by an attack of nerves—but most convincingly declared herself to be 'very taken', 'very impressed', '*very* taken', praise which endeared her more than ever to Josh, which might have been part of its intention.

Mrs Wilson would have said that of anyone Josh went out with, because she wanted him to be married. She wanted him to be settled, she wanted him to be a father, she wanted him where he would be safe because she feared that he was too easily led for his own good. Once settled, she said, his real nature would 'bring out his religious side again', rescue it from the shade it had been condemned to in the pursuit of selfish pleasures. No matter that he had been Church of England, she said, as long as it came out. It *did* matter, of course, that he had been Church of England, and one of the props in Mr Wilson's original defiance of the vicar had been the strength gained from his faith in the superior virtue of Nonconformity. Moreover, there was only the Methodist chapel in the village and Josh was not one to travel abroad to go to church—nor the type to split hairs about denomination: if Maureen could get him to the altar, she, later, could get him into a chapel. So Wilson's concrete offer was not without its loftier implications.

'How much is he asking for it?' Norman demanded as they debated the matter in bed about two months after the dance.

'Twenty-seven and six a week.'

'I knew it! Exactly how much your wages goes up by for being married! He should let you rent-free in that place, you'll be doing him a favour in keeping it warm.'

'It's a nice place.'

'It's a white elephant. Excuse me, Josh, but who's asked to live there these last few years? There's nothing modern in it. Not one thing.'

'It has electricity.'

'Don't be soft. What about a modern kitchen? That's what the ladies are after these days, not a scullery with a sink like a pig-trough.'

'I could do it up.'

'It'd *do* you to do it up and then he'd have done you again.' He was so pleased with that sentence he all but swallowed his stub. 'Bargain with him,' Norman ordered, who couldn't dispute the price of any article and never had done. 'That's what I would do. Beat him down.'

'The money I have in the post office could buy the furniture.'

'Don't be soft! Have you priced a bedroom suite recently? Eh? No change out of £150 there, lad, and that's nothing but the sheer essentials.'

'Mrs Wilson said she would give us some of her furniture and Janet's sister'll be selling up soon when they go to New Zealand.'

'Well I have yet to be convinced.' It would be just Josh's luck to land on his feet like that.

'What happened to you and Janet? You took her home that night.'

'Yes—I took her home.'

Josh did not press him; he never did and Norman resented it because this lack of pressure, this discreet indifference, teased out revelations which he would have defended and kept hidden under open questioning and did not want to be known.

'All right then. I took her home! I take them all home! Then they notice the grey hair or whatever and they're up the garden path like ferrets. Ffft! Bang!—That's the door. And good night!'

It was Maureen who took command; quite early on she discovered that she could, but there was no need to use authority at the beginning. Their love was equal then and made all else equal before it. She had not met such tenderness, nor reticence, nor lack of malice and viciousness, nor (though the word came out of a region distempered by disbelief) nor such goodness. And in those first few weeks the qualities were so new and so striking that it was as if she could hold them between her fingers like snapshots: yes, she would say to herself when remembering an evening together, he is gentle, he makes me so happy, he never wants to hurt me, he loves me, he is so good a man—and at that realization her heart, she believed, flushed with warmth as it had done before the altar after communion or before the brightly painted statue of the saints he reminded her of.

Yet you would not have thought, in those early days, that she was so in control unless you knew how relaxed command can appear, for mostly she was admiring Josh openly, and such pleasure did it give her that her wholehearted reaction embarrassed him hardly at all. And there were times, too, when she *wanted* to be *his*: to be at his feet; to be his slave, his servant; him to be her Lord and Master—for at times he made her yearn to love him so much.

One evening they were coming back into Thurston through the Showfields by the River Wiza. It was mild and still light and both of them were drowsily replete from having made love.

They walked by the edge of the river.

'We used to play there,' Maureen said. 'The boys would dam it up and make pools for us—and then the factory would send a man up to break all the dams because they need the water, you know, to keep it going.'

She liked to tell him about her past. It was as if it were endorsed and approved through his appreciation of it, while the atmosphere of nostalgia seemed appropriate to this gentle time.

'And the boys would pinch rope from somewhere and make swings from the branches. The thing was to try to get us to go on and then try to get us to fall off. There was only a few of us would dare to do it—most of the girls were too scared—most of them weren't there in the first place, of course, only us scruffs.' She smiled. She had balanced his being an orphan by declaring herself a scruff. 'That bit there,' she pointed to a gap in the bank, 'that was where Blister and our Tom blew it up with dynamite—fishing! They were drunk. They couldn't prove anything.'

Other couples passed them on this well-used courting route. And Cedric watched them from the distance he had set himself—somehow mitigating the indefensible nature of his enterprise by pretending he was brushing up on the tracking techniques he had learned in the Army on Salisbury Plain.

'What did *you* do?' she asked, 'I mean—for enjoying yourselves.'

'In the Home?' He stared away, abstractedly. 'Oh—there was always plenty to do.' He paused. 'The vicar, you know, was full of ideas for things to do. I worked in the gardens a lot—I liked that—they had a walled rose-garden there. It's been let go now. I used to go up and look after it, you know, even after I left the Home.'

'For nothing?'

'Yes . . . there aren't many roses as nice as you could get there. They had the old-fashioned stocks. But these new people aren't interested. They're going to clear it all with a bulldozer.'

'What a shame.'

'Yes—still, I might get a nice bunch or two out of it for you yet.'

'What else did you do?'

'Well,' and then, because he knew it would amuse her—he had told her before and she had been astounded by it, 'we used to have to keep the place in order, you know. Make the beds, clean the floors, lay the tables—'

'Lay the tables!'

'Yes. Wash the windows, see to the fires; then there was the garden, as I say, all the vegetables—it was nicc, having your own food from your own gardens.'

'Wash the dishes!' Maureen recited, to remind him. 'If one of my brothers was ever called on to wash a dish he would break the lot of them just to teach everybody a lesson.' She giggled to herself at this aspect of Josh. 'I haven't told them about this side of you, you know. They would call you a Mary-Anne and never give you a minute's peace.'

'Oh—they're all right, your brothers.'

He was looking at two young boys who were trying to vault from side to side of the river with a pole that was too long for them.

'Let's watch,' he said.

They sat on the grass despite the damp.

Encouraged by the spectators, the boys picked a fairly wide jump. One of them fell in, but the water was shallow there and he was carefully wearing wellingtons. The other could not lever himself high enough to get any swing at all.

Maureen could feel Josh's longing to have a go and the boys, too, seemed to sense it, or perhaps they encouraged it by their glances or enticed it by their incompetence, for in trying to pass the pole across the river, the unsuccessful one had succeeded only in throwing it into the water and now they were rather hopelessly rubbing it down with grass to dry it out.

'Did you used to do that?' Maureen's tone was half-teasing, but Josh replied seriously.

'Yes. There was a beck in the grounds. We used to pinch the poles Mrs Morrison used for her clothes-line.'

'Show him then. Go on. They'll be tickled pink.' How comfortable she felt in retailing his skills! No longer teasing, she added, 'I'd like to see you, anyway.'

Diffidently and in a manner which could not offend them, Josh strayed over to the pair.

'Could *I* have a go?'

'Can you do it?'

'I used to,' Josh said. He took the pole. 'It's a nice bit of wood. Just about my size. It's a bit too long for you, though, isn't it?'

'I told you,' one said to the other.

Josh took a couple of brisk steps forward and made an apparently casual jab with the pole which raised him gracefully and swung him easily over the water. Maureen felt her blood swoop with pleasure at the elegant power of the action. And Cedric decided to declare himself, coming down the small hill whose ridge had been his cover. Josh saw him immediately and waved him over towards Maureen: the two had met once, for a few moments, and shaken hands. Josh himself indicated another part of the river which was narrower and the two boys went along with him.

Cedric came and stood over Maureen. Each said hello and then they watched Josh teaching the boys to vault.

'Can you do that?' Maureen asked.

'No.' Sometimes Cedric got a special pleasure from telling the truth which did not reflect well on him—or rather from omitting to boast. He only did so in very particular circumstances—when he wished there to be nothing between himself and the other, nothing at all.

'Josh seems good at it.'

'He's good at everything,' said Cedric very tensely, his eyes never off balance. 'He has this balance. This physical balance. If you've got that you're in with a good chance. It's a gift, though.'

Maureen nodded. She did not feel like talking much to this rather odd friend of Josh's.

One of the boys cleared the river and Josh cheered. 'It's time we got going again,' Maureen stood up and beat at her dress, regretting her carelessness about the damp. 'Cheerio.' She moved away, leaving Cedric who had been planning to stay.

His eyes smarted suddenly and he walked away.

'Old Cedric pushed off quickly, didn't he?' said Josh, as they walked away from the dogged pole-vaulters.

'He *is* old, isn't he? I mean he looks *very* old to be, you know, your pal.'

'He's my best pal,' said Josh. 'He's great, Cedric.'

'You're getting soppy,' Beth warned her, 'kissing him like that when you're supposed to be dancing.'

'You used to kiss Jackie at dances.'

'Not like that. Not with my eyes closed and all that goo. It's sickening.'

'Just because Jackie's belted you.'

'Careful! You be very careful, my girl. By Christ! I'll be glad when we get out of this place and we can have a bit of bloody rotten privacy to ourselves, Jackie and me. And a punch in the eye isn't the end of it all, girl, even if it does look a bit blue. There's many a worse way to finish an argument. Then there's the making up—oh yes—you wouldn't know about that of course with Saint bloody Joshua. Never Puts a Foot Wrong, Joshua.'

'Jealous.'

'Why doesn't he have a bit more to say for himself? I mean —all right—he looks like something great—fine—he's the bees' knees—great!—and so on—we all love Josh: but he doesn't say much.'

'He never gets much of a chance in here with you lot arguing.'

'Who argues?'

'Some people only speak when they have something to say, you know. Some people.'

'Marriage'll do you good, my girl. It'll rattle your bloody teeth better than I ever could.'

It was when they made love that she saw her power and knew that she could use it. He was not afraid but nor was he insistent: he was not guilt-locked, but nor was he easy in his intention. He was a virgin and she was not. She liked his loving: she liked to be stroked as he stroked her, like the trail of his fingers on that tender inside of her thigh, liked his lips on her, his mouth, his body wrapped around her and she kissing him, holding him, guiding and directing him: she commanded his love as surely as she commanded every other important matter: she loved to lie back and let him go into her.

After the first time they slept together he had proposed to her most earnestly, no slip, no accident; and she had accepted, lightly warning them both to secrecy.

They had known each other for three months and were walking back into Thurston down the Longthwaite Road when it was finally settled. She had been quiet all evening but he never minded that and so had not questioned her about it, nor harried her at all. As they came to the first houses of the town they met a gang of little girls skipping with one end of the rope tied to a railing. They were singing:

> '*Manchester Liverpool Evening Post*
> *Ships are sailing on the Coast,*
> *England Ireland Scotland Wales*
> *All tied up with Monkeys' Tails.*'

Maureen was not three yards past them when she began to cry. There was no apparent stopping it as there was apparently no need for it; she kept repeating that as Josh put his arm around her in sympathy, 'no need for it', 'no need for it'. The little girls, aware, switched to 'Salt and Pepper' which they sang very softly as they strained to see and hear and know.

Maureen felt their curiosity and turned to glare, even at such infants, using the gesture to enforce her will and control her emotions. She dabbed at her face with a scented handkerchief as they walked down the hill and came to the entrance into the Junior School.

They turned and walked up the short drive which led to it: they were secluded and screened from the road and all domestic pryers. She leaned against the gates and looked at the neat, toy-like, bright red-bricked little school. 'I'm going to have a baby,' she said.

And Josh was jubilant.

CHAPTER SEVEN

CEDRIC was lost without Josh and it was quickly noted.

In the pub Bobbie Calthwaite began to talk about the Telford girls: about Beth and her reputation for being so hot—Passion Pants—Loose—Fast—Anybody's—Dying For It: and all the time, Cedric knew, he was really talking about Maureen and the others in the pub knew that too, he could tell though of course he was careful not to show it. He could feel everybody in the pub against him, all wanting to laugh at him. He knew how to deal with these situations.

'And they tell me her sister's not much better,' said Bobbie, by silence provoked to be open. 'That Maureen—that 'un Josh is after.' Winks and nods. 'He'll have told you all about her, eh? Cedric—Josh—he'll have told you about Maureen, eh? It is Maureen, isn't it?'

'Yes,' Cedric replied, turning to them. 'Josh's told me all about her. She seems a decent lass.'

'Pull t'other, Cedric. She'll be as easy to mount as a motor-bike.'

'She has some brothers as well,' said Cedric, being as ominous as he could, 'and Josh tells me *they're* not so easy to mount.'

'Josh tells you all that, does he?' Bobbie was just a little anxious. Word could travel fast; but this was too good an opportunity to miss.

'Oh, Josh and me tell each other everything.'

'Did he tell you he'd pack in training for a tart like that then? Did he tell you that?'

'His life's his own. We always agreed on that.'

'You should see your face.'

'What d'you mean by that?'

'Nothing. You should just see your face.'

'It's no good trying to work me up, you know.'

'Just *look* at his face. Your runner's run away, hasn't he? I bet Herb Elliot didn't scarper after every tart that showed him her knickers.'

'You know nothing about Herb Elliot so there's no point in talking to you about Herb Elliot.'

'Well, Josh'll be no champion now. Except on the job. Hey! Maybe old Josh'll turn out a champion banger—what about that, then? Has he had it yet, Cedric, has he told you? He tells you everything doesn't he?'

'There are certain things nobody asks each other; that's all I'm saying. Not even friends. Good night.' He drained off his Guinness. He felt cold with loneliness.

'Only *one* Guinness tonight then, Cedric?'

'He's away to meet Josh coming back.'

'Start training him on t' way from Thurston.'

'Poor bugger'll be shagged out to start with.'

'That's the word for it.'

'Oho, Cedric, your runner's run away and you'll never find another—'

'Watch it, Calthwaite,' said Cedric, at the door. 'That's all I say.'

He went out as they laughed at him.

Bobbie Calthwaite also worked at the quarry, in a dumper truck and all day beside him sat his mongrel Duke, a cross between a sheepdog and several sorts of spaniel. He would share his bait with that dog and though he didn't make the mistake which some did of taking him in the evening to the pub and so seeing him petted and spoiled, there was little he would not do for him.

Bobbie had never liked Cedric, never believed his stories, never liked his boasting, never been impressed by his travels; but nor had he challenged him outright because though he considered Cedric to be a common mixture of bluster and withdrawal, there was something vicious and hard about him which checked you. But here was a blade he could work into him! Bring him down to size now that he was back for good and driving that loading truck—just got the cushy job because the foreman had been in the Army for twelve years and was impressed by Cedric's references and his knowledge of regimental ways. 'Your runner's run away,' Bobbie would sing out. 'Your runner's run away and you'll never find another.'

Cedric made no reply: those who worked with him might have said he took no notice.

He knew how to get even and waited.

His plan was well worked out, but it needed patience and the effort involved in supplying himself with enough of it helped retrieve his mind from thoughts of Josh's betrayal.

He would have to come across Duke between about eight and nine when it was dark enough and there was enough time for him to do it and get into the pub for his usual drink. It had to be somewhere lonely. He had to be unobserved. He had to have a quick method and a convenient means of disposal.

He drew up schedules in the notebook in his bedroom and then burnt the paper they were written on.

And on the subsequent evenings he swept quietly around the district on his bike, keeping the engine low, thoroughly scouring the lanes and side-tracks, taking pains never to seem to be so conscientiously scanning the immediate neighbourhood, working out false destinations and filing suitable excuses in his mind. Beside Moorhouse Tarn one night he hid a sack and gathered a pile of large stones.

He saw the dog a few times and was friendly with him, but never at the right time. That would come. It salved the day's wounded pride and Bobbie's arrows were plucked out one by one as he thought of the effect of what he would do.

The evening came when he saw Duke on the road which led to the Plantation. He often went there and it could not have been better for Cedric who swept past him and around the Plantation, thus looking out for any possible observers (he had a fear that the vicar might see him and use the knowledge to blackmail him: that was his anxiety, blackmail) and also giving him the chance to shut off the engine and free-wheel down to where the fir trees began, where Duke might be expected to make for.

He turned his motor-bike around and put it on its stand, ready for a quick getaway. He knocked off his light and in the dusk took out the large haversack from one of the pillion bags. He opened it wide and set it on the seat: from the haversack he took a rope which had been looped at one end and a slip knot tied, making a lasso. Then he walked down towards the corner the dog must turn, looking about him every other step, trembling and tense but with no thought of holding back.

Duke came around the corner and Cedric dropped on one knee, fumbled in his pocket, was forced to take off his right gauntlet and stuff it under his belt. The freed hand brought out a piece of squashed fruitcake and he held it on his palm, sucking his tongue against his top gum, and alternating this encouraging noise with, 'Good dog. Here boy. Here boy. Here's a good lad. C'mon Duke. C'mon boy.'

The dog came up and ate and Cedric slipped on the loop of the lasso as a collar, using the length of it as a leash. He stood up and tugged only slightly, needing to encourage the dog so little that the animal could have been his own. They walked to the motor-bike. Cedric stopped and looked around. Listened with straining ears. The dog whined, in anticipation of more food.

Cedric took his time. No point in rushing this part. Oh—wouldn't Calthwaite be sick! Wouldn't he be screwed! All was clear.

He turned but just before he yanked the rope, a split second before, Duke understood. He spread his haunches, firming himself on to the ground, sticking his pads on the road, and ducked his neck, thus causing the rope to run up at that first pull and rest on the bone of his head. Cedric pulled viciously, intending to choke the dog in the first instance and while it was suffering, to swing it round and break its neck. Duke's action meant that the rope tightened but did not bite on the windpipe and when Cedric slackened slightly to let the rope slip back so that he could pull again, Duke leapt with the tension of the rope and was at him. Cedric's boot came up quickly and caught him a terrible kick on the side of the front leg; as Duke yelped, squealed, and dropped back, Cedric, thinking to be clever, reached out to knock the knot from the top of the dog's head. The dog snapped at his hand and bit deeply. Cedric stepped back, paused and then with a most violent heave, pulled so hard on the rope that the pressure could have broken the neck in one: but Duke had used the pause to snuggle his head further back; he slipped the noose and raced off.

Cedric switched on his headlight, all this time effing the dog for the bite on his hand where the skin was truly ripped. As soon as Duke saw the light he leapt off the road and scambled at the dyke until he found an opening which he was through and into the fields. It was pointless trying to catch him.

'Keep a cool head,' Cedric ordered himself. He could hear his heart beating and felt it threatening to stampede.

'Cool head. Follow instructions.' His hand stung and ached. He was afraid to suck it because of the possible dirt in the wound. With his gauntleted hand he picked up the rope and threw it into the pillion bag with the empty haversack. Then, still holding his wounded hand high, he got on to the bike. He needed both hands and felt brave as he pulled on the gauntlet. It was a time to move quickly.

At home his mother was glancing alternately at the *Cumberland News* and Border Television: when he asked her where the Dettol was it seemed to take her half an hour to assemble the necessary concentration. Sometimes, he told himself, sometimes he looked at her and then he thought of himself and that bloody maternal cord was about as strong as a bloody strand of thread. When she saw his hand she yelped, just like Duke, he told himself, gaining some comfort from that, and rushed off for the Dettol which he'd already put on. He let her tie the knot in the bandage.

He put on his black skin-fit gloves: real Spanish leather, he'd picked up three pairs in Gibraltar on the way back from the Far East years before. They were the Real McCoy: the Savile Row type of gloves—he'd wear them sometimes like a 'second skin' he said. He would have worn leather, real leather, all day if he could have had the sort of job that would have supported it. They were quite used to them at the pub so there would be no suspicion; he was in the pub by 9.45 as per usual. And a Guinness as per usual. And the crowd as per bloody usual. Bobbie Calthwaite, of course; old Hector Stainton, Wilf Rumney, Joe Haney, Dickie Robinson who'd been a champion swimmer in his day (and not long gone either) and his mate Maurice Johnstone; and the landlord, smiling Ernie Charters. One domino school (the first four), the two pals, Dickie and Maurice in desultory competition on the dart board and himself left to scan the field and occasionally pass a remark to Ernie. Ernie drove a coal wagon in Thurston through the day.

It was just after Ernie had shouted 'Last Orders' (there was no need to shout with just the seven of them there but that was his way) that it happened, the squealing at the door. Dickie heard it, went out—and came back to tell Bobbie that Duke was scratching half a ton of paintwork off the wood and seemed to need attention. Cedric drank off, watchfully. He could only leave through thc door which Dukc, it appeared to him, now guarded.

When Bobbie brought in the dog, Cedric backed away and Duke turned and bared his teeth in the most vicious snarl. His hair lifted and it tensed itself, ready to jump. Bobbie grabbed his collar. No one spoke. It was obvious to all that the dog had something against this one man and what was required was his explanation. Cedric guessed that the real truth would be so far from their thoughts that any old story told with conviction would serve to explain it all.

'So it was *you*, Duke,' he said, forcing himself to appear indulgently censorious. 'You silly old bugger. I could've bloody killed you—and myself for that matter.'

'How's that?'

'I was coming down the Plantation, see,' Cedric began, quite relaxed now, the entire story clear before him, the lie itself an attraction and a spur, 'and this bloody soft hound of yours comes out of a gap. Must have been after a rabbit. And can it go, Bob, eh? But I was on it, see? Right on it. You've seen tonight's roads—that bit of rain—I couldn't slap my brake fast on, see? And I felt the toe of my boot catch it—there'll be a bruise somewhere if you look for it. Bound to be—I caught it one hell of an effing clatter. When I turned round it was off. It *was* you, Duke, eh? They never get over it, dogs, do they? I've an enemy for life there.'

'I've seen that bruise,' said Bobbie. 'You must a' been travellin' at some bloody speed.'

'I was. I tell you, if I hadn't had perfect control and balance I could have killed it. Aye. Think on that, Duke, when you show your teeth at me. If it had been somebody else you'd a been a dead dog by now.'

'He is a bit stupid about rabbits,' said Bobbie, convinced, of course, as no reasonable alternative presented itself to him. 'And by Christ he has about as much idea of road manners as his maister has of table manners. Eh, Duke? Eh lad? But you're a tough old bugger, eh lad? Yes—you are, you are.'

Embarrassed by his emotional outburst, Bobbie left. As soon as he had gone, Cedric inveighed against the irresponsibility of dog-owners in general and the particular waywardness of Duke.

He was congratulated for surviving such an accident. All agreed that a dog flashing across the road in the dark was no easy obstacle. And, in a way, Cedric went out feeling himself a saver of life and a man of compassion and skill. The feeling lasted until he reached his own bedroom where he wriggled with pleasure at his own astuteness. Bobbie would call at him no more—he knew that: would think he'd somehow saved the dog. It was better than having killed it, he thought; in one way.

But his preoccupation was Josh.

'It's that I'm so restless just back from the Army,' he said to his mother. She rarely replied to him and occasionally he used her as a repository for confessions which were propelled into articulation by force of feeling and yet needed the protection of privacy. He would warn his mother against repeating certain things. 'You won't tell that to anybody, will you? Or I'll chop off your fingers. I will, you old baggage, don't think I'm joking. One at a time. With this knife. My mate used it to skin those Malays they caught in the jungle. He learnt to skin them alive from the Ghurkas. Every inch of skin off the man and him still not dead. I know you don't want to hear about it but you're going to hear about it because that'll happen to you if you tell anybody what I'm saying. You're my mother—right? So keep a secret or you've had it.

'Josh was something to concentrate on, see? I mean—in the Army you knew exactly what you were doing all the time, see? So much for effing drill, so much for bloody rotten talks; you ate just THEN, you had a break just THEN—see? There was some use in it. Not like these jobs in civvy street that do things at any old bloody time and interfere with the timetables laid down. We—Josh and I—we could—that training schedule was a perfect plan. Down to all the details it was perfect. I *per*fected it up in that bedroom, night after night. I've got all his times and the distances in a book—one blue, one red: and his exercises in a yellow one. All written down. Ruled and underlined. No half-measures.

'Now he wants to marry this bloody effing tart. She's got a face like a granite dwarf's and a mouth on her like a sewer-hole. She'll ruin him. That's all I say. She'll ruin him. She's tarted up scum; she's dressed-up dirt with powder on; she's nothing from the neck up and cheap from the neck down; she's a dragged up, bare-faced twat and she's got him in her grip. That's what annoys *me*.'

His mother knew better than to answer.

She observed that he was not looking well, but he shut her up. She herself was in constant bad health, forever threatening to leave him and take to the hospital, and he did not want to give her a legitimate excuse for talk of health. The way she talked about health made it seem a fantasy: always complaints and reports of others' ailments. But he gazed at himself in the mirror and pitied himself; perhaps he did have some mysterious disease.

He thought of leaving the district, but where would he go? He took up with Eddie Swales, another young man in the village, but only in a desultory fashion. Besides, Eddie was much more interested in his motor-bike than himself and could not wait for that time in the evening when he got his ride on it. Cedric could not be bothered with him.

'I'm a better man when I'm with him, see?' he told his mother. 'When I'm with Josh I don't feel like, you know the sort of things I do, breaking things—you know. I don't know what I'll do without him around. In the Army there was the discipline, see, you knew what was what. You did this—THEN! You did that—NOW! It was all laid out. But in civvy street—this ordinary life—I need Josh around to stop just—going, you know—like I did when I first left school.'

'You were only a bit wild.'

'You don't know the half of it you old—! I could've murdered people. That's why I went into the Army in the first place. I thought they'd just give me a gun and BANG! Kill the sodding lot. Da-da-da-da! Then I came across this discipline. Best thing that ever happened to me.'

There was something else which Cedric wanted to say but he wanted to say it direct to Josh. Not to spoil it by speaking it to his mother or to an empty room.

No one could have guessed his misery or his fury; they would have discounted the one and derided the other. 'You see, Josh,' he said, and his tone was most humble. He had waited on foot for the young man who had immediately leapt off his bicycle in a fine mood but, true to form, held it to himself and let Cedric take the centre. 'You see, Josh, it's difficult to know how to put this—but you were my mate and I feel I've got nobody now.'

Cedric was in his sports-jacket and ordinary shoes and the absence of the leather uniform underlined the beaten nature of his attitude and bearing. 'We were *really* mates. We would have done anything for each other, wouldn't we? We did everything together. There were fellas in our regiment like that but not me—not Cedric—I was too choosy. No—I'm telling you all the truth, Josh—there was *one* fella I palled up with for a time. When he got out I wanted to come out as well but my time wasn't up, see? But nothing like you. I mean—if you want my bike—you can have it—just say—for keeps—just say—straight—that's being mates. Maureen's nice—you've a nice girl there, Josh, and there's none speaks higher of her than me, ask anybody, ask anybody, just ask—but what I'm saying to you tonight is this: when all that's done with—I'll still be here to be mates. That's all I'm saying. Thing'll always stand with you and me, Josh, because that's it, see? You can't explain it—that's it. So; that's my meaning. I understand—it's buggered your training and ruined your prospects but that's a minor thing—the point is this, I'm always here. I just wanted you to have that straight—to have no worries on that score. I'll always be here for you, Josh.'

There was a pause. Then Josh put his arm around Cedric's shoulder, pressed it gently and, carefully controlling his excitement, said: 'I want you to be my Best Man. Maureen and me's getting married.'

PART TWO

CHAPTER EIGHT

ULLABY people were pleased that he was marrying, but sure he could have done a bit better for himself. Nothing stuck-up, but, well, that Telford family was a rough lot, there was no hiding it. Besides, what would she make of it in such a little out-of-the-way place? It was all very well living in Thurston with a coffee bar and shops and buses everywhere, dances and all sorts of do's and so on. Ullaby was cut off unless you had transport and they didn't even have a motor-bike. And she could say she was going to keep her job on and travel to Thurston in the school bus every morning, but that would need to be seen to be believed. What would she *do* with herself? A young girl like that used to so many people—so much to occupy herself with? Josh would have been far better off with a village girl—not necessarily Ullaby (though why not? Ullaby had brought him up, in a manner of speaking, and Ullaby girls could match any) but somebody used to peace and quiet and country ways, long winters and making do on very little. Mind you—she might be a Telford but she was smart. Smartly turned out. Well kept. Very smart indeed and they looked well together.

If he was happy—that was all that mattered. Aye, but would he be? He seemed it now—but marriage was a very different proposition, oh yes, marriage changed a few ideas, yes indeed, marriage needed a bit more than a laugh and a smile, that's right, marriage was a sickener for bringing you up against what was what! Yes.

They were married in a registry office late on a Saturday

afternoon in September. Josh had suggested that his vicar might marry them but Maureen would have nothing to do with that idea—she thought the old man was ridiculous and it would have made a laughing-stock of her wedding.

The nuns had been up from the Convent to get her to a Catholic wedding. They told her what would happen to her children if they were born outside the Church. Not being progressive, they gave it to her straight with much relish of hell and fire stirred by their own childhood memories of strictest Ireland and by the pleasure to the imagination which thoughts of Purgatory and the Lowest Regions always excited. Maureen was so upset the injustice of this fate for the unborn unlucky innocents should she not go through a lot of silly motions, that she 'went off the whole thing'. She had, she explained to Janet, been considering going back In: Josh would 'turn' if she asked him, she was certain of that, he would do whatever she asked. But all this Hell business, it was false and daft. A registry office would do for her and anyway she wanted nothing in a church two months pregnant.

Janet was a bridesmaid—she bought herself a new two-piece suit in pink. Cedric was Best Man and very smart in a black suit with a waistcoat and his regimental tie. Josh had got himself a midnight-blue suit at Penrice's in Thurston—only the very best—and a new shirt, light grey tie, new shoes. She herself had picked out his white carnation and pinned it in his buttonhole. He looked fabulous, she thought, and she was glad they had the public walk up the High Street from the registry office to Connolly's Café for the Breakfast.

Not a big party: Mr and Mrs Wilson on *his* side, and that loony old vicar had turned up, just *turned* up! and Norman, who'd really put himself out and bought them a complete tea service. Her family of course—they could look really something when they dressed up and were sober. All the men with carnations, the women with sprays and bags of confetti.

It was a proper wedding breakfast: cold meat, salad, plenty of scones and cakes, fruit salad and cream, sherry to begin, brandy for the men to end, port for the women, beer throughout. Her father always managed to get cash together to give his daughters a respectable kick-off, as he put it. He degenerated rapidly after the speeches, but then he wasn't needed any longer. Cedric's speech was easily the best. He read it and it was something *like* a speech, saying how long he'd known the groom and how lovely the bride was and thanking everybody on *her* behalf and so on: got it all in.

She had tormented Josh about the honeymoon until she had realized that she didn't really want one. She'd rather take the week off work *before* the wedding to get all ready and put the finishing touches to the cottage. (Norman had been a big help there: papering throughout, helping with the furniture. Both he and Josh treated her so politely compared with her brothers!—so worried when she lifted anything because of how it might hurt the baby. She revelled in their attentions.) Once she had thought of this idea, then it seemed so original that she was quite proud of it. Blackpool would just be a waste of money anyway, she said, and Morecambe was dead after August.

They would have the breakfast, go back to her mother's to change and so on, and then all of them have a night in The Thrush—which had a marvellous Singing Room since they had made the back end of the pub into one big space—followed by the dance.

'This is where we met,' Maureen said—she could not whisper, it was too noisy and she was a little too tight to whisper. 'That very first time. I saw you coming in and I said "That's *him*".' However often she repeated that, Josh would shiver with pleasure and melt to her. 'I *did*. Ask Janet, ask our Beth, ask anybody. And it was *me* had to make the first move, wasn't it? Mr Good-Looking wasn't looking my way, was he? "Should be looking my way",' she sang and held on to his neck with locked hands.

Blister came and tapped Josh on the shoulder. He was drunk.

'Let's have a kiss at the bride, then.'

'No, Josh.' Maureen clung more tightly: over-emphatic in her response—shrinking away from Blister in a way which could not have offended him more had it been calculated to do so.

'She doesn't want to,' said Josh, rather proudly and turned away.

'Oh no!' Blister held on to his shoulder. 'Fair's fair on wedding days now, Josh. Tell your little lady to give us a kiss. I mean—she's got to obey you now, you know, that's what they say, isn't it? "Love her and obey." '

'I don't want to, thank you. And it's Love, Honour and Obey, anyway. And nobody believes it nowadays so leave us alone.' Maureen was bothered by her own vehemence.

'Oh dear. Have I upset you. Oh dear.' Blister acted as if really concerned. 'Oh dear—now then—nobody need stand around watching! There's no trouble here. I'm sorry, Maureen.' Her face was in Josh's shoulder. To Josh he said: 'I knew Maureen before she was born—no, since, you get my meaning, pal? I know them all. And I can fight them all. But she's the canniest: you've got yourself hold of the canniest. I've always thought that about Maureen. And now she won't even give us a bit kiss. Won't even give old Blister a bit kiss when he wants to wish her "congratulations". It's not as if I'm asking for wedding-cake. I've had *my* supper at home—eh? Eh, Maureen—with Janey, *you* know Janey. Come on Maureen, just a bit peck and then I'll be off. What the hell, girl, you're *bound* to it on your wedding day. *Bound* to.'

'Maureen?' Josh nudged her, gently; her tense response admonished his over-accessible sympathy. 'She doesn't want to.'

'I wasn't talking to you,' said Blister, sharply.

'I know—but she won't say anything for herself so I have to tell you.'

'You tell me nothing, mister.'

'You asked her, though, a question, didn't you?'

'Look. What I say to people is my business and the people's business—nobody in-between—See?'

'She says no, anyway. So that's that.'

'And I'm taking no bloody "that's that" from you.'

'Sorry. Anyway. We want to dance now. Let go of my shoulder.'

'Say please!' Maureen was tense. Josh did not pause.

'Please.' She stiffened even more angrily.

'Maureen?' Blister tugged even more fiercely at Josh's jacket shoulder, and spoke very softly; 'Come on, Maureen—kiss-

kiss. It won't be the bloody first time, girl!'

'You rotten liar!'

'Aha. She's got a tongue. Right!' Blister let go of Josh and lunged for Maureen: his arms were about to go round her when Josh lifted him under the shoulders, lifted him clear off the floor and threw him aside. Then stood in front of Maureen.

'Wrestle you,' said Josh. 'Wrestle.'

He slipped off his jacket; his tie he had taken off long before. The carnation slid out of his buttonhole and on to the floor. He stepped on it as he stood back to give Blister room to stand up.

Maureen's brothers were among the crowd which had gathered—but so were Blister's.

'Wrestle,' said Josh: he stretched out his arms.

'Go on, Blister!' Go on, Blister!' 'Wrestle him, Blister.'

'You're supposed to be good,' said Josh.

Blister took off his jacket and they locked into each other, Cumberland and Westmorland style, both men as if they were bowing deeply from the waist, each resting his chin on the other's shoulder and then seeking to encircle their arms around the other's back, one arm under, one over. They would wait until both had a grip and then attempt to straighten up and throw the other. The bouncers came over with the stewards, but Cumberland and Westmorland wrestling was an accepted sideshow at such dances. Being without fists and confined to two and in the nature anyway of an exercise of local culture, it was not really considered to be fighting.

'I hope you murder him,' said Maureen who had put his jacket over her shoulders and was now guarded by Beth and her husband. 'I hope you break his bloody back,' she muttered.

The men crabbed around, each twisting and testing the other's grip. Josh was the taller man and at Blister's first attempt was nearly thrown. Blister snapped him upright like a jackknife in reverse and only by slipping down the grip did Josh prevent his overthrow. For a few seconds they stood, straining, upright together, body to body, intent on forcing the other to submit by the strength of the grip alone.

The band had stopped and were watching from the platform.

People rushed up and stood on chairs to get a better view. Norman, who had been exploiting his attendance at the wedding by pressing his interest in Janet, discovered himself next to one of Blister's friends, one who kept shouting, 'Break him, Blister; break him in two,' and he moved away. Cedric kept up a running commentary to himself: he had got stone-drunk in the pub but was sobered by the display. 'Look at his balance. With new shoes on. That's what nobody realizes. Come on, Josh. Hold him steady till you're ready. Eh? Look at that balance. Oh—oh—hold him. Hold him! Eh? Eh? Josh, you've got to keep a look-out for that buttock. He'll have you over that left hip. That's his game. Oh—Josh—hold him, hold him.'

Josh moved in so suddenly that the crowd were as astonished as Blister. He twisted him, half-straightened, lifted him clear while still in the other man's grip and then turned him over, breaking the grip clean as he stepped clear. If he'd wanted to he could have turned Blister upside down and thrown him so that he would have landed on his head. Everybody could see that he'd held himself back from that so as not to break his opponent's neck.

Blister was on his feet instantly. He sized up the situation and saw there were times when you had to play the sportsman. Josh was an unknown—there was no real humiliation in being thrown by a non-starter like Josh who was no fighter and had no reputation; and of course he had slipped on that chalky floor.

'The best man won,' said Blister, holding out his hand, and he felt the murmur of surprise, relief and appreciation lap over him warmly. He had done the right thing. 'Well done, pal.' He insisted on the handshake, though he noticed that Josh was not enthusiastic. 'The best man won,' he repeated.

Cedric thought that he might be crying with the emotion of it all. He pushed his way through the crowd to the Gents. The band started up, the stewards moved people on, Blister strolled off, Josh received the congratulations of Maureen's brothers. He'd given them real value for their sister. Beth took Maureen off to the Ladies Cloakroom and Norman produced his half-bottle of brandy which he insisted on Josh sipping at.

'I'll be your trainer, tonight,' he said. 'This'll keep you fit.'

Josh only sipped. He'd had enough to drink for that day. He put on his jacket and, forgetting he had a tie, turned his shirt collar over the jacket collar. On the floor he saw his trodden carnation. He picked it up carefully and slipped it into a pocket.

CHAPTER NINE

Mr Wilson said nothing and tried to pretend that he was astounded; but really, he was very curious. What had made Josh turn? Surely just getting married could not have such an effect on a pliant soul like his. He sat to one side of the window and twisted to look out at the dusky Saturday afternoon; the light caught his grey hair and whitened it. It was a mark in the dark room, unlit, deep in sombre colours as if all had been darkly varnished, the silence somehow compounding the twilight and the broad table, the heavy chairs and massive fireplace giving weight to the whole; even the fire did not flicker but merely eased out its smoke through a pile of slack which had been banked on it hours earlier for economy's sake. Josh sat across from Mr Wilson, even his blond hair subdued by the room's sobriety; only his hands sometimes caught the light, large, chunky hands, red, uncouth, out of true with the rest of him. Behind him, unmoving, in the rocking-chair beside the fire, the only one of the three who was aware of the full drama in the occasion, Mrs Wilson sat and waited for her husband's reply, her eyes dimly peering; spectacles were a sign of age.

'Well, Josh,' and still the farmer could not bring himself to look the young man in the face, 'I must confess that you've taken me by surprise. Thirty bob! Thirty bob over and above the twenty-seven and six. Dear me, Josh.' It was as if the sum made him embarrassed—as if he could not not look at the other man because he had breached good manners so tastelessly.

'It'll just make me level pegging with the married man at

Pattinson's,' he said, addressing his fingers.

'Oh! You've been discussing my business with him, have you? That's *very* nice!'

He turned into the room and looked at the top of Josh's bent head: his turn let in the light and it caught the fair hair which held it from then on.

Mr Wilson leaned forward earnestly.

'You mustn't listen to others, Josh. The Good Lord gave you a mind of your own to make up for yourself. I know all about that married man at Pattinson's. Nelson they call him, isn't it? Eh? Frae Scotland! Take no notice.'

Mrs Wilson saw the young man's shoulders set: it was neither a shrug of anxiety nor any nervous shuffle of the muscles but a definite squaring up. Despite her disapproval of this challenge to her husband's authority, Mrs Wilson felt a trickle of excitement, so positive and active a thing that she wanted to sneeze—but she rammed a forefinger on her upper lip and censured the act.

'You see,' this came from Josh fumblingly; he had learnt the piece by heart but wished he had not, for the business of trying to remember made it appear false: the hesitations, the wrong accentuation, as if he were speaking lines written for him by someone else—and so what had been honestly felt was invalidated in the delivery. He sensed this, and yet the importance of the occasion made him cleave to the formality.

'You see, we've worked it out—Maureen has. When it's all worked out, what we'll need, and nothing to do with extravagance, I'm going to do part-time bits for extras next spring and summer: this is what we worked it out to.' It's Maureen's put him up to it, Mrs Wilson thought, in some disappointment.

'What part-time bits?' Mr Wilson was truly put out. '*What* part-time bits are you going to do, eh? Is this another thing you've been discussing with that Jock?'

'No.' Josh spoke carefully, still, determined not to be thrown off his path. After all, Mrs Wilson thought, wishing him to find strength, it was no small thing for him to challenge this man whose orders he daily took unquestioningly.

'I've just asked about. There's plenty wants an extra hand. I can do it after I've finished here.' Asked about: *she* can't have had anything to do with that, Mrs Wilson thought, happily: she would not know there *was* such work.

'*I'll* employ your spare time,' said Wilson, jealously. 'Come to me before you ask about. I can give you extra to do.'

'But I want paying for it, Mr Wilson. And with you it would just be part of my job, wouldn't it? Like that fold I've been at this summer. There's many an hour I've done overtime on that but there was no extras.'

'I never asked you to go over your time.'

'But you said it had to be done.'

'Only if you could manage it. I never ask for what's impossible.'

'There's only two of us, Mr Wilson, with you away now. I had to work late at it.'

The farmer stared, sternly, at his tightly clasped hands. It was true that he was away much of the time these days. Having been a hard worker in his youth and then a driver of others, he was taking a rest, would disappear in mid-morning, mouthing white lies about stock and auctions and agents, and motor around the countryside at his leisure, stopping at some remote and cheap café for a snack. Mrs Wilson did not torment him with this evasion but she appreciated the ammunition it gave her and occasionally sent out a shot to show her potential firing power. He was worried that word might be getting around.

'Well, that's as may be. There's more to running a farm than driving a tractor but nobody appreciates planning and paperwork in this locality. No wonder it's so backward, everybody pinching everybody's else's labour. You come to me if you want extra, my lad. And as a matter of fact, about that sheepfold, I was going to include it in your Christmas bonus so no more of that.'

'It doesn't bother me, Mr Wilson. It's just I can get paid, you see, by others.'

'You'll get paid by me. I'll meet you half-way, Josh. Fifteen bob a week extra and every hour extra you claim I'll pay you overtime for.'

Mrs Wilson savoured her husband's shrewdness. By putting the onus on Josh to claim for the extra work, he was undoubtedly saving himself a few shillings, maybe a great number.

'I'll ask Norman to add up the hours for me then,' Josh replied. 'I would make a mess of it.'

Was he prepared for that offer then? Whichever way she looked at it, Mrs Wilson was impressed and she rocked, just slightly, on the chair, to express her pleasure. If the girl had put him up to it, more power to her—but it was Josh who was doing it—looking at Wilson now!

'Oh! So you'll have another man come into it.'

'Norman—yes.'

'I see.' He nodded and shook his head slightly but violently, as if thus to dislodge the painful thought.

Mrs Wilson would have given a year of her life to disturb the balance of the afternoon, get up, walk across and plunge her fingers into that glowing crown of blond hair.

'It'll have to be thirty bob. I'm sorry. I can't—we can't manage on less.'

'And if I say no?'

'You've been very good to me till now.' Josh looked up cheerfully and smiled at his employer who welcomed this break in the inexplicable tension which had been growing hard in the dark room.

'Aye, Josh. We've got on well together, haven't we?'

'Yes. I wouldn't be half as contented anywhere else. You and Mrs Wilson have been very good. She's been wonderful.'

She held her breath, not wanting to disturb by her presence. The mention came as praise, all the sweeter for being uttered so earnestly and most probably in a moment at which he had truly forgotten she was there.

'Aye well, she's a fine woman,' said Mr Wilson, who had observed his wife's reaction and, being himself moved, made conscious of a way to see his path through this business without losing face; for he could trade on her affection.

'She'd want me to help you in any way I could, I know that,' he continued, not unaware of the treasure he was piling up for himself in her account, 'so I'll tell you what I'll do. I'll put a pound on straight-off. And I'll set aside ten bob against this overtime you'll be doing—there's no question but what you'll be worth it every week. So how about that?'

It was not quite right but it would have been churlish to refuse and ridiculous to have gone through further arguments for what after all would amount to thirty shillings a week.

'All right; thank you very much.' He stood up, moving out of the light, and turned to Mrs Wilson. 'I wouldn't have bothered you, you see, but Maureen'll have to give up her job soon . . .'

'. . . when the baby comes,' Mrs Wilson concluded for him. 'There's some eggs in that bucket beside the door,' she added, rather too hastily. 'Take yourself half a dozen.'

'Thank you.' He smiled and went out.

The eggs were newly laid, unwashed, still the damp earth on them and bits of straw tangling the slightly sticky surface. He took out his handkerchief and placed the six eggs in a careful pile. Brown ones. Maureen had this funny partiality for brown ones.

'They should make out well if he's as determined as that,' said Mrs Wilson—for although she realized that her husband had made a concession and understood that she had had some influence on that, their relationship did not tolerate mutual flatteries or congratulatory intimacies.

'Any man who knows his own mind is a step nearer truth,' said Mr Wilson, adopting the ways of a preacher, which was his habit at heightened moments.

'Nobody could work harder for his good luck than Josh,' his wife returned, sonorously.

'He's making a palace of that cottage anyway.' There was some reproach in this. 'Still—I suppose it's his home.'

'Yes.' The door banged: he was gone.

Mrs Wilson stood up and moved to the back-kitchen to put on the kettle for tea. She had been remembering Josh before her own fire, the numberless times he had kept them company, the richness of his presence and how it pulled at her whenever he left. She had to give him presents now, whenever she could, tokens, remembrances from one home to another messages, links.

Through the window she saw him cross the cobbled farmyard, carefully holding before him the white handkerchief heavy with the eggs.

And it was a palace he imagined himself going to on that bleak northern afternoon. Never had he had a house of his own; never even a room of his own; nor felt the lack. But now, with a wife, he had to have a place of his own and in the possession had discovered a deep source of pleasure. Since Cedric's departure—he had left Ullaby soon after the wedding—the cottage had taken second place only to Maureen and even she used to affect to be rueful and tease him with complaints about loving their house more than he loved her.

If he had not been carrying the eggs he would have run. Usually he did run. People noted it with some relish, tinctured by envy or nostalgia according to their own memories. Today he wanted to finish painting their bedroom: he had even raced back there for half an hour at midday to put on another roll of paper. Saturday was a short day and he had a double advantage over Maureen because she both worked an hour longer and took advantage of the extended Saturday bus service to visit her parents for an hour or so after her work.

It was when he got to the cottage, as now, and shut the door behind him—there!—then what a jet of happiness gushed through him! He leaned against the door as if tired from some strenuous physical effort and looked around the kitchen with such intense pride as needed thick stone walls to confine it. Each object seemed more wonderful than any similar object anywhere. That table which Mrs Wilson had given them had never looked a tenth the table before but now, with those four saleroom chairs—almost a perfect match!—what a table it looked! He could have sat on a chair, his elbows on the table and dreamed of meals to come, of games around the table, of just sitting there. And the travelling clock on the mantelpiece—a present from Beth—went so well with those two ornament things, china bunches of flowers, one at either end, which an old lady from the village had sorted out for him: he went across towards them, first putting the eggs on the table and rubbed his thumb lightly over the delicately moulded clay. That picture of the Blessed Virgin Mary and Child which one of Maureen's brothers had given them—it *made* the far wall and somehow the frame matched the furniture. Everything fitted in.

Sometimes he would stand there in what might properly be

called a waking dream, just weighing what he had, breathing it in as if it had been the most odorous perfume, his eyes resting on the simple furnishings with the self-hugging pleasure of a collector enjoying a rare piece, listening to the rest of the house and bringing it before his mind's eye, room by room—all re-done by himself, papered, painted, mended, plastered, fixed, wired—he had slaved in that place only just able to prevent a total eruption of joy by driving himself to labour.

There was a song they always used to sing, the Salvation Army, at the corner of Water Street and King Street on Saturday nights when he and Norman used to go into Thurston to the pictures—and the words would often come back to him now as he filled himself with the knowledge of the overwhelming fact that this room was his, was where he lived, where he and Maureen lived and sat and spoke and were man and wife, where his children would live—that was the secret of secrets! —his children-to-be—think of that!—he could think of little else, he who had known neither mother nor father, neither brother, sister, cousin nor anyone called relative would have a child, made by Maureen and by him. Someone from himself who really belonged to him—and here, in this place was where it would be. He shouted for mad happiness as he pulled off his jacket and thundered up the stairs—what a thing it would be! this family, this house, a father to children, nothing, nothing he had known, not even his love for Maureen had intoxicated him as this thought did and he prepared the place as for the coming of kings—'Running over, running over'—that was the song.

> *'My cup's full*
> *And running over.'*

He began to sing it—loudly and tunelessly

> *'So the Lord save me*
> *I'm as happy as can be*
> *My cup's full*
> *And running o, O, O, O, O, O—ver!'*

When the time came to make the arrangements for the birth, Maureen half-persuaded herself that it was Josh's love for the house which led to her decision to have the child there. She hinted so, then wished she had not because his response was so overwhelming—it was wrong to move someone so much by a lie; but later she decided that it had been only a white lie because the turning of the bedroom into a small maternity ward with the consequent fuss and concern occupied her and flattered her—and she absolved herself completely, remembered his reaction guiltlessly.

The fact was, she had been put off by the alternatives. She had gone to the clinic for her pre-natal check-ups and felt squeamish; the clinic was attached to the out-patients' department of the hospital and hospitals upset her. No one in her family had ever been in hospital and they were proud of it for they feared it as the entrance to the grave. And the queueing, the breeziness, the lack of privacy offended her who had always held most stubbornly to a private lot despite the marauding of a large family. Then there was the Catholic place—but once again though a solace in prospect, in practice, when she went there to look around, she was angry at the righteousness of the Sisters; their very existence made her feel unworthy and the thought of herself being powerless before them was unendurable.

When her mother—who had had all her children at home for some of the same reasons as Maureen—promised to come up and help, she was confirmed in her decision and reassured. And when she discovered that a midwife would be provided and the local doctor was likeable and conscientious, she felt she had gained an advantage through her squeamishness and obstinacy. She moved the picture of the Virgin and Child into the bedroom.

The labour was long. Josh sat beside the bed whenever he was allowed to do so by the ministering mother and midwife. He held her hand and tried to think of things to say. Sometimes they played cards—Snap or German Whist. He was quite overawed by what was happening before him. Maureen's presence rushed into every part of him like the sea flowing over a beach. When she took his hand and placed it on her belly he could have fainted—so powerful was the drug of emotion which was released. But this sense of wonder, of potently confused feeling, a rich mixture from all his most piquant and treasured experiences and desires, stayed calm and untroubled.

The pain had lasted for over twenty-four hours when the doctor decided to give her some knock-out drops, as he called them.

'You need your sleep, my girl, before the big push, eh? The great leap forward, eh? That shove we're all waiting for, but you're tired now, you've been a good girl all day but there's no use forcing it, as the mother said to the boy whose head was stuck in the railings, so we'll dab you there, relax, good girl, now this won't hurt a bit and it won't hurt baby, just give you both a rest before the cup final, there we are, a kind of half time, there, didn't hurt did it? Now lean back, close eyes, yes, we'll be here when you come back, cash on delivery, that's right, yes, sleep, yes—good. She'll be out for a good five hours and I'd get myself some shut-eye, young man, or we'll have you in bed too. Call me if she starts at the water-works.'

Josh went outside. He was exhausted but he did not want to sleep. It was about five in the morning, pitch black this late-winter time and still. He walked a little way up the village to keep himself warm and came to the Barn. In its doorway he sheltered from the wind and prayed for Maureen and the child, prompted and comforted by the former nature of the building.

When he stopped it was once more the stillness which struck him. He welcomed it. Swiftly it passed through his exhaustion and his anxieties and his prayers to that central self which had always sustained him so serenely and now pulsed with anticipated joy. He wanted the silence. It came to help him; and out of it, out of the winter-crusted earth, from the covered burrows and sheltered holes, from seed and sanctuary, from within the calm would come that life which Maureen too would give. He breathed deeply, sucked at the chill air, wanting to help pull out its life.

He decided to go to Carlisle and buy her some roses. He saw them clearly in his mind, thick velvet red petals, dark and rich, enfolded luxuriantly, sprigged with leaf; and dew-drops singly settled on them.

There was a shopkeeper called Gilbert Little in the next village who at one time had gone to Carlisle Covered Market, every morning, for his fruit and vegetables, and Josh had heard him speak of the flowers. He could bike there in less than an hour—longer back because mostly uphill but nothing more than an hour and a half. That gave him plenty of time in hand.

He jogged back to the cottage. The midwife was dozing in the chair beside the bed: she approved of his plan—though he went into no detail, merely saying that he wanted to get her a present at the market—and she reassured him about the five hours and promised to keep his secret. Maureen looked so beautiful. She lay asleep as if posing, her face so sweetly angled, her hair so well displayed. Her mother had brushed it before herself retiring; brushed her sleeping daughter's hair as if preparing her for a party. Josh would have liked to kiss her but he did not care to in front of the midwife.

He set his watch and wound it up.

Down from Ullaby, his front light cutting through the dark like a razor through cloth. Top gear most of the way; just under fifty minutes it took him and his face was tanned hard with the cold.

The market was along one side of a triangle formed by the Castle, the Cathedral and the Town Hall. He had expected noise and crowdedness but the streets were uncluttered; a few vans, fewer lorries. He propped his bike outside, next to a street light, and went into the huge cold hall which echoed to footsteps and sentences which sounded irritable in that vast chilly space. He saw nothing before him but rows of shuttered stalls. He walked towards where he thought the sound was.

The small group of people who were unloading and organizing themselves seemed so self-contained that Josh hesitated before going across to them. As far as he could see, no one was buying anything. He glanced at his watch and went across.

'Excuse me, missis; sorry to bother you. Could you tell me who has flowers here, please?'

A woman fat and stiff wrapped in many layers turned and pointed.

'Sharpe's,' she said.

He went in the indicated direction and then saw the name on a van.

'Mister. Are you Mr Sharpe?'

'Aye.'

'Could you sell us some roses please? Red.'

'No roses today, lad. Daffs I've got. Tulips from the Scilly Isles. All that you can see in that van, lad, but no roses. Too much risk for me, lad, in Carlisle. Excuse me, pass that box while you're standing beside it; thanks. Take her some multi-coloured tulips, lad, and she'll love you for life.'

'I was told you could always get roses here.'

'Aye well. Talk's cheap, lad, and roses is dear. Pass that other box, eh? Thanks.' Josh handed him the box and then automatically continued to help Mr Sharpe while he considered what the best course might be.

'I'll tell you what,' said Mr Sharpe, when all the boxes were passed over, 'I'll do myself a bad turn. There's John Ford comes in a few minutes and he always brings roses on principle.'

'How long will he be?'

'Oh, John's never later than about half past six.'

'About twenty minutes.'

'Aye. Time for a cup of tea. There's a body with a stall round this back end. Coming?' He turned away and then turned back. 'Freesias?' Josh shook his head.

'Come and get some tea then or they'll be using them roses for your own funeral.'

He would still have plenty of time, he thought, and a cup of tea would be welcome. He felt rather giddy—the hot tea would steady him.

'Hurry up, lad, there's my missis.' Mr Sharpe dodged around the corner to escape his wife and Josh paused, rather slow in his reaction, and looked at her—she nodded and her expression was sweet.

'Go on for your tea,' she said. 'He likes company.'

She began to take the flowers out of the boxes and put them in green buckets which were in front of the stall.

'I'm looking for roses,' Josh said.

'Oh. I thought you were a driver. John Ford has roses.'

'What time does he come?' Seeking reassurance.

'Six-thirty. What's the occasion? Don't be shy—I can always tell—it's, you've just been made a father, haven't you? Roses at this time in the morning. I know. Your first? Well. Boy or a girl?'

'It isn't born yet. The doctor gave her an injection. She'll sleep for five hours.' In this meagrely populated place, so shuttered and cold, he was anxious. He might have cut himself off from her. 'Do you think I should've left her?' he asked.

'Where is she?' Mrs Sharpe was pleased to be concerned; to be in sympathy with others, to feel for them was "a gift and a blessing", her mother had said—And it was often very helpful to the business.

'We live in Ullaby.'

'Oh—it takes no time to get to Ullaby.'

'No.' Josh did not care to refer to his bike. 'Do you think she *will* sleep?'

'If the doctor said she'll sleep then she'll sleep.'

He nodded, miserable and unconvinced. Quite suddenly his action appeared to him to be stupid. He ought never to have left her.

'I think I'll go back,' he said.

'Now don't be so *nervous*,' Mrs Sharpe smiled mischievously at him. 'It wouldn't do to go back empty-handed, would it?'

'I'll buy her some grapes.'

'They're very poor this time of year.'

'Well, those freesias'll do.'

'No. You came for roses and you must stick to roses—you'll only be disappointed if you don't.'

That was true.

'Get yourself a cup of tea. He'll be here in, let's see, about ten minutes.'

'No. I'll wait here for him.'

He went across to one of the stalls and squatted in front of it. Mrs Sharpe talked to him now and then, though he could have wished she would leave him alone. From where he was he could see the large white face of the clock which swung from the ceiling and twanged its iron pointer from minute to minute, stabbing its way through time.

Mr Ford arrived just before the half hour. Mrs Sharpe let him get out of the van and open the back door before shouting out: 'There's a young man here to buy roses'—her arms outspread she pointed at both of them, joining them in herself, that gesture of hers at once hoisting Josh to his feet and turning Mr Ford away from his van. He sized up his potential customer instantly.

'They're five shillings a bloom,' he warned.

Josh was shocked.

'Half a dozen then,' he said, as he walked forward; he had about two pounds and had hoped for a dozen. 'I'll take half a dozen.'

Mr Ford clacked his tongue in irritation. He was always prepared to bargain a little over such prices. The fellow had no sense! If he had waited a few moments and even seemed to be worried he would have made some interesting offers. And there was Mrs Sharpe glaring at him as if he had robbed the young man. It was most aggravating.

'They're for his wife,' said Mrs Sharpe, sternly. 'She's about to make him a father.'

'Ah well. We always do a special price for births. I can do twenty-five bob for the half dozen or, let's say, two guineas for a dozen,' he looked at Mrs Sharpe for her approval; that reduction had been made solely to reinstate himself in her good opinion. 'Or, let's see,' he went on, not wanting to dwell on the latter figure too much, 'I'll give you seven for twenty-eight shillings or——'

'That—that'll do—seven.' Josh's throat was dry. He longed to go. They would never stop talking, these people. It was stupid of him to be here, listening. Maureen could need him. She could be awake. The pains could have started again.

'Please,' he appealed to Mrs Sharpe who saw the panic and nodded.

'Don't keep the young man waiting,' she said, 'there may be a new face waiting for him in Ullaby.'

'Ullaby is it?' said Mr Ford, with interest. 'Do you know a Lawson in Ullaby?'

'Yes.'

'And—let's see—there was a man there used to show at the County Agricultural with me every year. He had the next stall. They're arranged alphabetically, you know, and so it must be near an F. Indeed it could *be* an F—but I can't exactly bring him to mind. Short fellow; fair. Well, more grey than fair but still some fair. What *was* it now? *He* could grow roses.'

O God! Josh stood helpless before this man. O God!

'Would it be Gordon?' Mrs Sharpe asked, giving Josh a quiet smile to reassure him that the digression was well under control—but finding a name to fit a face, a memory, a fact or an action was even dearer to her than confidences.

'No, no. You're thinking of Adam Gordon from Little Bampton—no: different fellow altogether. Adam Gordon *is* fair but—no. I'm sure it was F.'

'Franks.'

'No.'

'Featherstone.'

'No, no, Mrs Sharpe.'

'Sometimes if you say what comes into your head, it helps. Foster.'

'Foster! Yes. You should go to him for your roses, young man. But not in this season of course—eh?' He too smiled: both of them seemed to find real satisfaction in smiling at him.

'I've heard of him,' said Josh, quietly. 'I'd like my roses if you've got them, please. I want to get back to my wife, you see.'

The polite expression of what yet appeared as intense longing chastened the chatting pair.

'I'll be as quick as I can,' said Mr Ford.

'Some fern would go nicely with them, let me give you some fern—for baby's sake,' and with the last phrase she once more reverted to her compulsive searching for the crack of sympathy.

'I'll bring my bike in. Then I'll be ready.'

He walked away rapidly, glad of a chance to ease the worry.

'A bicycle!' Mrs Sharpe called after him. 'Do you mean a *bicycle*?' Her words were swaddled in sympathetic delight.

Josh pretended not to hear. What a fool he was, he thought, to have come. Fool, fool, fool to have left her!

'Josh.' He stopped, seized to a standstill, startled: it was Maureen's voice saying his name, as she had said it after the last bout of labour pain. 'Josh, Josh,' so weakly but so sweetly trusting that it had pierced him to tears which he had been unable to resist. 'Josh, Josh.'

He walked quickly and then ran out of the building. He had come out of a different door. More lorries were arriving and one threatened to back into him. His reactions slow from the fatigue and the confused tension, he was forced back into the market and had to wait until it had dragged its inching length between the doors.

It was almost intolerable.

When he turned the bike he discovered the front wheel was buckled: slightly but badly enough to make it unrideable. In those narrow streets which reflected more faithfully the period of the thirteenth-century Cathedral than the Victorian Market, a lorry must have nudged it. He pulled at the wheel, straining to mend the damage with his hands. Though the rim yielded a little, he had not the strength to restore it.

By now the need he felt to return to Maureen was a pressure which threatened to overwhelm him.

He leaned the bicycle against the wall and went to some men unloading a consignment of fruit.

'Has anybody a hammer I could have for a minute?'

'What for?'

'My bike. There's a wheel needs straightening out.'

'Just a minute . . . Harry! Harry!—bring that hammer out of that bag beside that bait tin, will you?' The request was shouted into the market-hall and eventually it was answered by a small boy who carried the hammer aggressively and seemed disappointed that it was not he who was to use it. He accompanied Josh and watched him attempt to tap out the dent.

'It's your spokes'll have suffered most,' he said, the choirboy pitch and tone of the voice contrasting markedly with the weary accent and wearily adult manner of speech. 'They'll have been weakened—I can see three of them gone from here—it'll need money spending on it to get it right.'

Josh concentrated on the job. 'It'll take me where I want to go,' he said.

He spun the wheel. 'There.'

He got on the bicycle and pedalled a short way: there was some bumping but nothing unmanageable.

'I still say your spokes are dicey,' said the gloomy boy.

'*There* you are! There he is!' Mrs Sharpe pointed at him as if she were singling out a pick-pocket. Mr Ford popped out from behind her, carrying the roses in a polythene bag. They were red as he had hoped, dark red. And when he saw them, his interest in them revived.

'*I* suggested the polythene,' said Mrs Sharpe. Josh pulled out his money. 'Young men can't make parcels,' she went on, 'and once I knew you were on a bike I realized they had to be well protected.'

'Twenty-seven and six . . . Thanks. I knew you'd give me thirty. Here's your change.'

'You get to know what to expect in the way of money,' explained Mrs Sharpe.

The boy had been scrutinizing the spokes, poring over them, hammer in hand, inflicting the occasional tap. 'You'll surprise me if these stand up to more than a mile,' he said.

Two or three men had drifted up, drawn by the faint scent of an accident. Josh looked around at the unknown faces and had to shut his eyes.

'Are you sure you're fit enough to ride back?' Mrs Sharpe asked him. 'I'm sure I could find somebody going near enough Ullaby who would give you a lift later on—not *much* later on,' she assured him insistently, wanting her help to be accepted, prepared, even, to promise what she could not be sure of performing in order to exercise her staunchless kindliness. 'There's plenty goes that way—you'll see, they'll have you back to hearth and home in two sniffs of a cat's whisker. He's about to be a dad, a new father,' she announced to the small crowd: there was a mutter of understanding. The small boy walked away.

'Thank you but I'll go,' said Josh, 'I'd rather.'

The men moved away.

'It would be no trouble for somebody,' Mrs Sharpe laid a hand on his arm, as if imploring him, 'they'd get you there faster and safer and he does look tired, doesn't he, Mr Ford?'

'Ah well,' said Mr Ford. 'We none of us look our best at times like this. Good morning and good luck to you.'

Mrs Sharpe was left alone. She felt her isolation and was very conscious of her hand on Josh. It was taken away as if it had met with a slight electric shock.

'Thank you for wrapping these up,' said Josh, 'it was very good of you.'

He stood the bike still for a moment while he took a tight grip on the flowers; he would hold them pressed against his chest, steering with one hand only.

'You really should have had a cardboard box,' said Mrs Sharpe, rather mournfully. Then her suggestion caught her fancy. 'I'll get you one.' Once more she bustled. 'Stay here, I'll get you a cardboard box. I know where there is one that will be just big enough. We might have to trim the stems a little—but . . .'

'I must go, missis: I'm sorry.'

'Now, do as you're told! How will she like her flowers all crumpled.'

'I'm sorry missis; I can't wait any longer. Thank you.'

He pushed himself away and began to pedal.

'Tie them on the handlebars!' she shouted, waving goodbye with black mittens. 'I've some string here—here in my pocket.' She pulled it out and waved that, too. 'Go carefully—it's a nasty corner that . . .'

The wind came from the north-east and blew him along the plain but it was bitter. A vein on the back of his right hand—which gripped in the middle of the handlebars—began to swell and he was forced to stop and suck it, then to beat it to restore the circulation.

There were few lorries; it was not very light. The cold was slapped on to him like a skin which drew tighter the more he strained. His legs were heavy and he felt the drag on his muscles at each thrust of the pedals.

When he turned off the main road to go up to Ullaby he was met by a cross-wind and by now there was a sick feeling in his throat and his stomach. The bicycle meandered from side to side of the deserted road as he pushed against the wind and the gradient. His hand ached badly: the vein was a lump.

It would be easier to run.

He opened a gate and pushed the bike behind a hedge where it would be safe enough and then began to jog up the hill. After a little while, some warmth came back to him and the pain in his legs eased. But not the dense push of fear which pressed against his skull.

'Up-two-three-four! Up-two-three-four! Come on, Josh—get them effing feet off that tarmac—Up-two-three-four!'

He stopped and shook his head to throw off the memory of Cedric's voice which came as clearly as if he had been there beside him. He walked a few paces—looking up the fells towards Ullaby. He breathed in dccply.

'Through your nose! Breath through your effing nose. That's what they do. Get the pure oxygen out of it. That's what your blood *needs*—see? Now then—away we go—come on! Up-two-three-four! Up-two-three-four!'

Josh began to run again—faster this time, as fast as he could, pressing the roses against him as might have been a cross. He heard the engine of a motor-bike behind him and the sound momentarily horrified him. He turned. It was someone from the village who stopped and nodded and Josh climbed on behind him.

When the baby was born, he was deep asleep downstairs in one of the armchairs. They did not wake him until all had been washed and tidied.

Maureen was sucking at some small green grapes when he went to see her; the midwife had arranged the roses in a large cut-glass vase and they stood on the chest of drawers in front of the picture of the Virgin and Child, obscuring it.

PART THREE

CHAPTER TEN

THE child was really too small to be left alone, but people in the village were used to that now. And, being a village, there was always someone to keep an eye on her—or so the more anxious reassured themselves, for the child was already a general favourite. She was startlingly like Josh. His hair, his eyes, his complexion, his smile; and she moved so gracefully, flitting, like a butterfly—stopping quite suddenly and then lightly moving on—several caught that similarity—just like a butterfly. 'Poor little thing.'

They always added that. There would be praise and wonder, real pleasure and delight, then 'Poor little thing'. The bolder oncs added 'What d'you expect with her mother being—like that?' But it was better to leave things unsaid and most confined themselves to commiseration.

Anne, she was called, almost four years old now, their only child, Anne the name of the mother of the mother of Our Lord, Maureen had said, and would have no other name.

On this calm and summery afternoon, clouds high and light bowling from the Atlantic to the Continent with no time to pause over England, fells stirring with sheep and some few tussocks of drying hay, the Solway glittering there on the plain like a chastening sword between Scotland and England, and the plain itself from the height of Ullaby appearing sleepy and peaceful and richly secure—there on the small hillock behind the chapel, the little girl played. She wore a blue dress and sandals. She was collecting daisies, making ropes of them to hang around her neck and put on her head. For such a small child she was extraordinarily nimble and self-contained. Maureen had seen her go out into the back-field and then had put up her feet to enjoy a read. She had given up work after the birth and only occasionally and temporarily gone back to it. If she wandered to the door from time to time, that would be enough. Besides, what was the fuss? Anne always came back. Josh would notice her if she was to be noticed at all; he seemed to plan his day's work on the farm to make crossroads with his child's day.

Today he was at the funeral of Cedric's mother and it was on the burial that the child looked down as she went to the far side of the hillock. She picked out her father and waved her arms—shaking the daisies tempestuously.

'Daddy–Daddy–Daddy–it's me—Anne. Me—your Annie. Dad-dy.' The thin, sweet voice rang clear over the last mumbled words of the preacher and people smiled, though discreetly. Josh waited for an Amen to give him cover for his move towards her, his expression proudly remonstrative above the cutting white collar and the black coat.

She was in the churchyard before he got to her and she dodged behind a headstone as he reached out for her, so abrupt and light-footed her movement, so sweetly mischievous her eyes, that his heart lurched with tenderness and his efforts to catch her were mistimed, thus making it appear to her that a game *was* being played, for he could always catch her when he really wanted to, easily.

'Come on now, Annie, come on now.' The words were muttered, reverentially, as his feet stumbled against the hump of the grave. The words from the prayer-book went on.

'Daddy! Daddy!' Her voice sang, so light and tinkling in tone. She raced across to a large tomb which leant to one side in its first ruin.

'Look for me, Daddy! Look for me!' She hid herself behind it, then peeped out and laughed.

For Josh was walking as he sometimes did in playful pantomime with her—taking large, menacing steps to pretend to frighten her. She laughed with a thrill of cosy fear. She could not know he was intent on avoiding the graves.

'Please, Annie. Please, my love.' Still his voice was church-low. 'Come to Daddy.'

The preacher no longer smiled. He was an old man who had six villages to care for and the Methodist Church was not rich. There were times when it was very hard to be poorer than your poorest parishioners—or as poor, must not exaggerate. He stopped to embarrass Josh into effective action and, taking their cue, thc fcw mourners assumed expressions of some annoyance. Only Cedric showed no sign, staring blankly at his mother's coffin in the opened earth.

Josh seized his daughter too hard, in his eagerness, and hurt her arm. She cried a little—more to have the comfort than express the pain which had left almost as quickly as it had come—and he lifted her up, making a seat of his right forearm which she liked, and said 'Ssshhh' while he turned to watch the last moments of the burial.

The chapel itself was no longer used but it was this particular type of Methodism Cedric's mother had followed and they still made use of the cemetery.

The preacher left with the mourners and Cedric stood back to let Mr Pape get on with filling the grave. There was to be no tea, no 'occasion'.

Cedric turncd towards Josh and looked most deliberately at him. Anne waved. Cedric lifted a hand and came over.

'Let's walk a bit together,' he said.

Josh nodded. Anne clung to him as he tried to put her down and he knew it was better to keep her where she was than set off the trouble of parting her from him. She would be quiet enough while they talked.

They took a path which led around the hillock and came round upon the village by way of Ismay's farm.

This was Cedric's first visit home since leaving Ullaby. He had joined the Merchant Navy.

'They brought me back as soon as they heard about it. They flew a mate of mine back from Christmas Island once and got him back in time. It's one of the things they do—get you back for this sort of a funeral. They guarantee you that.'

Cedric had arrived the night before. A neighbour had seen to most of the arrangements. Cedric's mother had saved up carefully for the funeral and planned it herself. There had not been a great deal to do. Josh had gone to see if he could help, but even the coffin-bearers had been taken care of; she had not wanted local people. The firm would supply bearers if you asked them and she had set money aside for that also.

This was the first time the men had talked beyond a greeting, since the older man's return.

'Are you long back?'

'I was at the end of my effing—pardon'–to Anne–'spell anyway. This compassionate counts as days and finishes it off. I might sign on again. I don't know. I'll have to think about some things. That cottage might have to be sold. It'll fall apart if it's not lived in.'

'You look well, anyway.'

'Oh, I'm fit enough. *You* look a bit—peaked.' Cedric noticed Josh's strain at this first meeting; his face was tense, the eyes wary, the young man's whole attitude and expression out of true with his former character. Cedric had not had the time to discover any reason for it. He knew it would be useless to ask Josh. He thumped him hard on the back and Josh's head almost bumped into Anne's face.

'It's this married life takes it out of you—eh? Got any more where she came from?'

'No . . . only the one. Anne she's called. Anne—this is Cedric. Cedric and your daddy used to be good friends.'

'Used to be?'

'You've been away for such a long time.'

'Some things don't take any notice of time, Josh. We're still friends, Anne. Here.' He produced a wallet and took a pound note from it. 'That's for your drop-box.'

She took the note and held it carefully. She smiled at Josh who returned the smile and then she pushed her face forward, turning the cheek to be kissed. Cedric walked on, not noticing.

'Say thank you,' Josh whispered.

She repeated the two words and Cedric nodded approvingly.

'I said I'd be back for the milking,' said Josh. 'I shall have to be away.'

'We can have a drink, can we? I mean—tonight.'

'Are you . . . ? Will you want to with your mother . . .'

'She can't mind either way, can she? I'll be in there from eight.'

'Right.'

'Have you any transport?' Cedric shouted after him. 'We could go somewhere else, then. After we've had one here.'

'I've a motor-bike,' said Josh. 'I'll bring it.'

Cedric nodded and then he climbed the hillock to the donated seat where he placed himself for the next half hour, watching the grave of his mother taking shape and trying to calm the excitement of a confusion he thought he had left for ever long ago.

The matter had become so well-known that it was difficult to get the full story. Besides, Norman's usual part in the talk about Josh was to take his side, either by extravagant loyalty or by threatening the speakers to silence. Even a simple account appeared a betrayal.

'Why are you so interested, then?' Norman asked sharply. 'You'll just be here today and gone tomorrow.'

'I was his friend, wasn't I?'

'That was long ago.'

'He came to my old lass's burial. You saw that.'

'Yes,' Norman replied. 'Well, his missis, his wife that is, she's, you know, she and . . . remember a fella called Blister—Thurston fella, mean?' Norman could go no further.

'Maureen and Blister?'

'Now nothing can be proved! I mean—Blister drops in to see her but it's well known that he's friendly with her sister and he might just be passing messages and same reasons apply for him taking her out in that old car of his. I mean she needs covered transport to get to see her family and you can't grudge her it. Besides, he works in the quarry now and he's bound to bump into her and anyway he was one of her lot and she'll likely want to hear all the gossip about *them*—we *all* do about our own. And apart from anything else, is Josh the man to let there be any of that going on without making a carry-on? He has a temper, Josh, even if he does keep it to himself. And no wonder the lass wants to see somebody, anyway, for all the notice she gets taken of her in this place—coming from Thurston she *must* find it a bit of a let down. Look into your *own* hearts: that's what I always say.'

Cedric loafed down the road so as not to be obliged to go into the pub. He was no longer confident of his position: could no longer menace the place. He wanted to be somewhere quiet. He wanted to sort out this situation: he repeated it to himself like a prayer, 'Must get it worked out. Must work it out.' He still wore the black coat from the funeral. It was new. He had bought it in London on his way back. 'Must get it worked out.'

Josh came down the road steadily, at no great speed. He drew up beside Cedric who got on the pillion.

'What's that for?' he asked, shouting above the engine.

'The side-car? That's for Annie. I take her out with me. She likes the old motor-bike.' Josh smiled at the empty side-car. 'Where to?'

'Let's go well away. Up Hesket. That way.'

Cedric put his hands lightly on Josh's shoulders as they went along the narrow roads. The sunset was intensely dramatic —half the sky streaming with reds and pinks, mauves and pale copper, the colours being sucked into the gorging sun which was poised above the horizon, unwilling, it seemed, to sink out of sight until its greed had been satiated.

CHAPTER ELEVEN

He often went out shooting now when Annie was in bed or in Thurston. Maureen took her there every Sunday afternoon. Blister picked them up in the car because it was weatherproof and anyway more dignified than the motor-bike and side-car which looked comical, these days, and old-fashioned, however useful. He would watch them go and wave at Annie's white, fluttering hand rubbing on the back window of the car and then he would get his gun. He had no dog. They had got a pup soon after Annie's birth but it was too messy for Maureen's taste and she had insisted that he get rid of it.

The Sunday after Cedric's return followed the pattern. Blister arrived at about half past two. He had been drinking in Thurston until two when the pubs closed. Josh had once tried to persuade Maureen that Anne would be happier spending the afternoon with himself; rather unfortunately he had put it in that way without, as he might have done, disguising it by emphasizing how much more convenient it would be for Maureen, how much more of a rest. He was no match for her. She had told him that the child's grandparents longed to see their grandchild and, as she knew it would, that ended the matter. Anne was decorated with her best clothes and brushed and washed for viewing.

Blister would honk the horn and stay outside. If Josh came out he would nod, from inside the car, and shrug despairingly, hoping to transmit a feeling of disinterested impatience which he tolerated only because of his good-neighbourliness. When Anne appeared, he would give a wolf-whistle and push open the back door of the car. She practically dived in, loving the bounce of the springs. Maureen would come out with a preoccupied air and always turn back as if passing on some final confidence to her husband. Once in the front seat, she would rummage in her handbag, her eyes resolutely down, until they were well out of Ullaby.

People often chauffered others. There were still a number in that district who were without cars. It was not exceptional.

Josh went out by the back door, over the low wall at the end of the garden, and up alongside the hedge which concealed him from the village. There was a wood on the other side of the hill, more a scattering of copses, really, but you could pick up something there, from time to time.

He went past the old castellated building near the quarry and round the rim of that deep crater to get over the hill. Once among the trees, he leaned against a birch trunk and waited.

Cedric had found out about this Sunday routine and was prepared for it. His cottage was conveniently placed; from a back bedroom window he could see across a short field to the Thurston road. He had asked, casually, the make of Blister's car and he took up his position at two o'clock to be on the safe side. He had a hip-flask of rum which kept him company; he had become used to it in the merchant navy and tales of nights of riot on rum were already seeping into the village pool of gossip.

He saw the car come. He waited. He saw it go. He went out and up the village to Josh's house.

When there was no reply he walked around to the back door. It was not locked. He went into the house.

As he said later to Josh, he was very worried from that first minute of going in. You could tell a well-run house, he said, by the feel of it; and this felt wrong. It was tidy enough, in a way; but when you'd been in the rotten Army and served in an effing ship, my boy, sod it! He'd seen the dust where others would have missed it but a good wife wouldn't have missed it. Oh—it was tidy enough in its way but—the dinner plates weren't washed up for instance, they weren't even cleared from the table. Now he could understand a woman in a rush not having time to wash them up, but no woman worth the name would leave that clutter out on the table for people to come back to. It made the rest look worse than it was. There was nothing you could put your *finger* on—though there again, he'd gone upstairs to look around—he knew Josh wouldn't mind him being interested in the house aspect of his life; after all he would have been *shown* around it if Josh had been there; he'd worked on that basis—and the bed was so badly made! Do it like that in the Navy and they'd stop your rum! He'd felt like stripping it and doing it over himself. He'd almost started to, in fact, and then remembered where he was.

Little things like that.

When he came out of the house, Cedric went to the bottom of the garden where a makeshift shed served as a garage for the motor-bike. It had been firing badly when he and Josh had been on it. He wheeled it out into the side-lane, kicked it into life and listened. The faltering was still there. It was not difficult to find Josh's tool-kit.

He set himself to locate the fault and repair it. As long as he stayed near Josh he would not hate everything, he thought. He wanted to stay in Ullaby now. He was too old to be in the navy or anywhere away from here. But he had to be careful; he would no longer get away with his tricks. Somehow, Josh would make it work.

The vicar knew where Josh went. He made his way up there in a leisurely manner—Sundays were always tiring. He'd spend the night with the police in Thurston station and they'd drive him back to Bothel for the eight o'clock communion but he'd generally find himself walking from Bothel to Ullaby and exhausted when he got there. To get up in the middle of the afternoon was to make a special effort, but it was called for, he thought. He'd watched Mrs Tyson's funeral and seen the meeting between Cedric and Josh and Anne. It was the time for him to have another talk to Josh anyway. The man needed help. He looked badly and it made you grieve to see someone who had been the expression of happiness looking so beaten, his cheerfulness coming through such strain that it scarcely broke on to his face.

Josh had killed a rabbit and it huddled against the base of the tree in the arm of a surface root. The vicar sat down beside it, spreading out his raincoat and inviting Josh to share it. But the younger man preferred to keep standing and make a pretence of being still interested in shooting.

'It's bad for *her*,' the vicar said, going straight to his point. 'You stand back and let her have free play with this man. Josh; it is a husband's duty sometimes to be firm with his wife. To say no. "With my body I thee worship"—yes: but that's got nothing to do with criticism. And criticism must be part of it.'

The vicar paused to allow Josh his turn. But there was no reply. There was no indication that he had even been listening. The vicar was used to this and kept on the path he had taken.

'There are some people who are weak and some who are strong. Our Lord was both kinds of man. He was crucified because of his strength and in his weakness he cried out, "My God, my God, why hast thou forsaken me." That is why we can learn from him—he presents all things to us. Both sides of the case. "Made flesh and dwelt among us." Once there was flesh there was weakness and we can have no sight of the glory in these earthly lives. Just intimations.'

'Josh: I am speaking about your wife. She is in a weak position. She left her Church; she left her town and her friends to come here with you. She cannot or she will not keep her job, she will not have more children.'

'Neither of us wants more. Neither of the two of us.'

'Well. That doesn't affect my main point which is that she doesn't stick at things. And so you must keep her to them. When you brought her here as your wife you took on a responsibility and you must carry it. And part of responsibility is the unpleasant part. That's why people avoid it. There often *is* this unpleasant part and if you've taken the responsibility in your pride then in your humility you must face the unpleasant part. You are not doing that, Josh. You must tell her she is wrong: you must tell that man not to see her again: and you must try to understand that she is a lonely young woman up here. In fact she might be very lonely and that makes people frightened, I know that. I suffer from that. It is most distressing. The more distressing because it is not like rheumatism or a broken leg, not something people are used to giving their sympathy to; but it is every bit as crippling as either of those, believe me. Lonely, frightened people are lame. I have some idea of how she might feel.

'I think it might even be a good idea for you to go and live in Thurston.'

'I couldn't live there.'

'Why not?'

'I don't know—but I won't go there.'

'That is pride, Josh. That is putting yourself before another whom you have sworn to love. What matter if her man lives there? All the better to settle it with him. What matter if you know few people there? All the better to start again.'

'I couldn't live anywhere but Ullaby. I wish I could. But I can't do it.'

His voice was sad, low and desperate. The vicar let a silence soothe the air between them before going on. 'What do you intend to do, Josh?'

But this only prompted more silence. They were there, the old straggly-haired man with his grubby dog-collar and cheeks aflame with health, the veins reaching out at the surfacc of the skin, threatening to break through, and the young man, jeans tucked in wellingtons, old loose jacket, cap, pouch, gun slung half-ready under his arm; in the wood, under a slate sky, and between them the dead rabbit, smudged with blood at the neck, the fur stiffening.

'You see,' the vicar began afresh, 'you mustn't talk of what you can't do. That's how people hurt themselves. You can't like what's going on. I know you, Josh, better than you know yourself. And if you keep yourself away from a decision, you'll do yourself harm.'

Josh spoke without turning to the vicar, spoke quietly as if detachedly. But he was tired, such talk tired him. 'A child needs a father and a mother,' he said. 'You've got to have a family. Nobody can break that up.' He paused and then added, desperately, 'Whatever anybody says—you mustn't break it up.'

The vicar stood up and dusted at his trouser-seat. Despite

the coat, damp had penetrated. 'You need to talk to somebody sometime. You can always talk to me.'

'I don't want to talk.'

'There are worse things than breaking up a family, you know. Better that than breaking the people in it.'

'Thank you.'

'I know *you*, Josh. You're too concerned not to hurt anybody. I'm convinced that if you had this out with Maureen she would begin to see sense. She's not a bad girl. She's lonely. I can see that. Talk to her.'

Josh moved away, pretending to be attracted by some glimpse of wing or fur. The old man had seen the expression on his face and left him alone with his grief.

Blister could not keep his hands off her. She excited him when she stood, when she walked, when she turned her face towards him, when she shrugged. When she left a room it was empty, when she came back in it was flooded with the fullness of her body.

In her mother's house he went upstairs to finish some papering he had been doing for them. He had undertaken it obviously and solely for the purpose which was now pursued; for Maureen brought him up a cup of tea and on the bed they locked into each other, groaning quietly, clothes scarcely disturbed, each caught in the intensity of the other's need for passion.

'He never gave her enough of the old You-Know-What.' Beth spoke of Josh very sympathetically when Maureen was around. But when her sister was upstairs and they had to pretend not to notice the shuddering ceiling and keep an eye on Anne to see that she did not go upstairs, she found her true assessment to be that which most safely kept the afternoon on an even keel. For her parents were against it all; they had never got on with Blister's lot. 'Well, it's true,' she defended herself against the embarrassment which her directness provoked in the Sunday-afternoon kitchen, the men in suits and the afternoon long with the later opening time for pubs.

'I think if he'd been, you know, half-decent, our Maureen would have been happy to put up with him. Because she liked him—I mean—who couldn't like the lad? She *still* likes him—yes—that's there as well.'

Beth had tried to help her younger sister on several occasions. She was quick to pull out the real difficulty from the pride and evasions of the younger girl; and she wanted to help.

'Look,' she would say. '*Tell* him. Tell him not to be frightened. It's up to you, my girl. If he's worried about hurting you—well, that's very nice of him. It often happens after there's been a baby.'

'It was smashing up to then. *He* was smashing up to then. Really! But since then—he's—I think he's—you know. Since I decided to have no more.'

'And quite right! Quite right!'

Maureen had never dared tell about the contraceptives. She had insisted on them after the birth of Anne. Josh was too embarrassed to buy them. It was not even clear to Maureen whether or not he was fully aware of what they were. Norman who missed him at nights and used the previously quiet meal-breaks to unload his conversation and feel out the friendliness of the man, had stumbled on to this embarrassment and, without saying a word to Josh, bought a packet for him and, casually, sold it to him—out of sight of anyone. Josh hated them, however, and would not wear them. Maureen was afraid of him without them.

Beth had soon found out about that.

'It's up to you,' she had said to Maureen. 'The bugger's supposed to look after you—that's *his* side of it: but you've got to tell him what you want. That's yours. And if you're missing out on the You-Know-What—tell him. Mind you, there's thousand never even get a sniff.'

'But I can't!' Maureen would repeat this again and again. 'He's not that sort of a man. I can't talk to him about things like that. It would worry him—I mean he's such a good sort of man. Sometimes I think he doesn't *see* bad.'

'There's no need for anybody to be blind, not about personal matters.'

'I'll try.'

Maureen did try. Sometimes she felt that Josh was longing for her to succeed; but whenever she looked into his face, the purity of his look abashed her. She felt ashamed for all the wrong she had done before she had met him and for every single bad thought since. She was in the state which the thought of St Teresa had once induced in her as a young girl. Josh, when he slept in that cosy leather chair beside the fire after supper, with his hair so blond and skin so fine, would remind her of the statues of the saints they had had in the class-room; something in his expression. Anne certainly looked like a little angel! But those were the sort of thoughts you began to have alone in that cottage with all the old women of the village just waiting for you to put a foot wrong.

Blister was such a relief; and such a pleasure. Her nature rode its coarser roads to greet him and stamped on the more tender ways.

He drove up to the door, as usual, and let them out without leaving the car himself. He would be back into Thurston for the pubs' opening. She'd tried to encourage Josh to drink to get him out from under her feet sometimes. But though he went, obediently, it was reluctantly that he left the hearth.

She did not wave to Blister but went in, looking neither right nor left.

In the middle of the table was the dead rabbit. She edged around the table warily and then bustled to the back door, almost knocking over Anne in the process.

Josh was in the side alley with Cedric, watching him re-assemble the bike. Anne instantly ran to the wall and lunged at the top of it in an attempt to scramble over.

'Get that damned rabbit off my table, Josh Lawton! You *know* I hate the things. You *know* I do.'

He came to the wall and, leaning over, held out an arm stiffly. Anne clung to it and swung herself backwards and forwards.

'Sorry. I didn't expect you back so soon.'

'I'm always back at this time.'

'We got caught up in mending the old bike.'

'Well, leave it and get that stinking animal out of my house.'

Josh nodded and raised Anne up on the one arm. He slipped her on to his shoulders and then swung himself over the wall and went towards the house.

'We'll take it up to Mrs Wilson,' he said to Anne. 'She likes a rabbit pie. You can see the new chickens.'

Anne clapped her hands and then ducked, giggling with pleasure as her father's similar motion caused her to seem to topple forwards. Even so her head bumped lightly against the frame top of the door.

Cedric had followed Josh to the wall and he stood there, rubbing his hands on a rag.

He looked amiably enough at Maureen but said nothing. She did not want to go back into the cottage until the rabbit was out of it.

'I was sorry to hear about your mother,' she said, eventually. 'It must have been a shock.'

'Yes.' Cedric was momentarily solemn. 'Still, she had a good life.'

Maureen was straining to listen for the bang of the front door.

'Will you be staying for long?'

'I don't know. Maybe I'll settle down here now. There are worse spots.'

The door banged. She smiled, brightly, at Cedric, nodded and went back into the house.

CHAPTER TWELVE

Josh must be upset to be so careless about the rabbit. He respected her likes and dislikes. He did not tease her about her squeamishness as her brothers did, or even Blister did. He must be upset.

She clattered through the dishes rapidly but efficiently. Concentration on one thing helped her with another and she was keying up her courage to attempt a confrontation. She was the one who would have to begin it! Maureen grumbled to herself about this while sluicing the plates under the cold tap; just like him to want to say nothing, just like him to wriggle out of it when she started it, she had always to be the one to take the decisions, like now about leaving him. It was for his good, his own good, far better for him. It was no good either of them being a laughing-stock and she was sick of people using her for their dirty-minded conversations. She was doing nothing she was ashamed of. Nothing at all. Everybody can make a mistake and hers had been Josh. Better say so and be done with it. Better clear it up—however hard that might be.

She had tried before.

The thing, is she muttered to herself, he's done nothing wrong. I mean what can I say to him? I'm the one who's supposed to be doing something wrong and yet it's me has to point it all out to him. He should be throwing *me* out. Then I would know where I stood. If only he'd do something bloody wrong for once. I have more against Blister than I have against him. I can find fault with anybody at all except Josh. But I won't have it. Why should I stay here if I don't want to? He can't force me to stay. Not that he does. But he loves me and it'll be terrible for him if I leave. So why doesn't he try to stop me? If I do get round to telling him, that is; will he? I must tell him though. I can't stand this two-timing. It's not fair on me. I'm the one that has to do it. Nobody takes that into consideration.

Sometimes she said to Blister when he was taunting her and prying into her privacy to discover exactly what went on between Josh and herself in bed, sometimes she'd say: 'If only he was my brother! You know. I can't think of anybody I'd rather have for a brother—or a friend. Or just somebody to be fond of.' And Maureen felt distinctly elevated when she said that, as if she were calling up some sacred part of herself to cope with this unwanted situation and had surprised herself in finding this holy attitude; for it *did* surprise her, to be so moved to such an odd declaration. Blister, of course, would get mad and tell her she didn't know what the hell she *did* want.

She wanted him. She wanted Blister. If just for those seconds of rough, violent taking, of a passion drawing on childhood fantasies and secrecies; if only for that.

The trouble with Josh was that he was too home-loving. Put Annie to bed and all he wanted was to sit and wait for her to whimper so that he could go upstairs and cuddle her some more. Which was all very well for a bit. But there were limits! Just like the way he always—he *always* agreed with what she said . . .

This berating his blameless shadow never got her very far. Invariably she ended up imagining herself to be wicked, who could be so ungrateful to someone so loving.

She sat in her chair in front of the fire and watched the television. She sucked at her cigarette and tried to feel as bad as she had learned she ought to feel. What would Father Kelly say? And Sister Pat? And Mother Superior? She ought to shake to think of it, oughtn't she?

She was not entirely successful at feeling evil. She was too nervous, waiting for Josh, because some stubborn point had been reached which could not be evaded. She *had* to tell him and break away from him.

I'm glad that Cedric's back, anyway. At least he'll have a real friend to turn to when it does happen. That's something.

Stirring uneasily in the battered armchair, she waited, and watched the religious programme.

Annie was in bed.

Josh was mending one of her toys, a small wooden truck, yellow with four bright red wheels. He sat on the black rug before the fender. The heat from the fire could have been scorching his skin, but he did not appear to notice. The blond hair swung down over his brow to his eyes fixed on concentration on the blade of the knife with which he was cutting new sockets for the wheels.

The television was on, but low. It was a film which Maureen had seen before. Josh had watched the first few minutes and then ignored it. Maureen wanted it on for the sound, there was some comfort there. She was ruffling the Sunday newspapers, making a point of her restlessness, attempting to disturb Josh even into mere irritation which would give her a note to start on. But he concentrated on fitting the red wheels to the yellow truck.

How secure she had been, once, in his imperturbability! Content just to sit there in the silence of that cottage away from family and job and chatter of Thurston, knowing that all before her belonged to her.

She knew when it had changed. Annie had changed it. It was too late now but once she could have hated her for it; a little girl, her own child—except that you couldn't hate children. But after Annie had come, he had changed entirely towards her, she thought. The business of not wanting any more had been her idea but still . . . nobody need have been that disturbed—if you could call it disturbance—*hurt*, more like. She knew it was hurt. Hurt in his eyes with her irritability when he came in from work so happy and vigorous and herself exhausted with the feeding and washing and fending for the child; hurt in his stiff, tense body when she pushed him away from her in bed; hurt when he told her how sorry he was about her stitches—she blamed herself for telling him about the stitches—hurt when she began to demand times of love and ways without his desire or mood, and yet he would try, the love, and she would feel his affection dragging after his duty, would feel his body sullen despite the willing words; even in the dark could see the smitten look in the eyes.

Then Blister had teased her and taken her one night at Beth's. So easily.

Since then she had been waiting for the hour to tell Josh, willing herself to tell him. She had her plans made. She would move into Thurston and live with Blister and his mother. Annie would very soon be old enough for school and the infants' place there was good. Josh would not *really* be alone; he could go back and live at the farm and anyway Mrs Wilson would always cook for him.

Her shame had grown greater the longer she had allowed time to pass with the truth unstated. For her own sake it needed saying. She was only twenty-two! She wanted a bit of happiness. She could go back to the factory when Annie was at school; her mother would collect the child. And she wanted more fun. Anybody could make a mistake.

Why should she be writhing in her mind in this God-forsaken village, pinned to a cottage kitchen for life by a man whom she could only hurt and hurt while he put red wheels on a yellow truck? She could have screamed and howled in agony, spread her arms and thrust herself up, claimed some notice of the world with all her force—and in some fundamental way, she thought Josh would not *really* care. I can't seem to touch him, she had once said, with a mixture of wonder and pride. Now it was a desperate sentence.

But there was so much cosiness here. And so much that was right and *good.*

She thought herself very bad because he made her want the things she knew were wrong. But she longed for rows, verbal cruelties, petty transgressions and boasts of violent enterprises, the build-up of tensions for release in fearful actions of intense, sentimental loving.

'It's so quiet here,' she said.

There was no sign from Josh that he had heard her. Carefully, using the action to help shape her feelings, she reassembled the scattered sheets of the Sunday newspaper and folded it tidily, smacking the pages into place.

'What made you bring that rabbit in here?' she asked.

'I thought you would be back a bit later.'

'I was back at the usual time.'

'I got tied up with Cedric. He's fixed that rattle.'

'You know I hate dead things like that.'

'Mrs Wilson says she'll make a pie for next weekend.'

'I won't eat any of it. She spoils you, that woman.'

'She's a good boss's wife. She's been good to me.'

'It's the least you can expect. You'd work yourself blue for them.'

'No I wouldn't.'

'You know what I mean.'

'Wilson's an easy gaffer.' For the first time during these exchanges, he looked up and directly at her, so intensely that her exasperation fled. If only he would follow up that look— 'I've been thinking about that rabbit,' he said, 'for Annie. What I could do is dry out some skins and stitch them up into a sort of pouch for her. She would like that. She likes that book with Maid Marion in it. I would put a big wooden button on it and tell her it was just the handbag Maid Marion would have had herself. What d'you think?'

'As long as you don't bring the filthy things in here.'

'I'll clean them. I'll leave them to soak overnight. Fur's no problem.' He paused, then smiled at her, secure in another loving preoccupation. 'I'll get to work on that,' he said.

She squeezed the newspaper into a large ball and threw it on the floor. It landed next to the truck.

Josh looked up again and waited.

'We must talk about us two, Josh.'

Again there was a pause. She saw him as if encased in glass; he moved, at these pressing times, in lakes of silence. Which she could not endure.

'There are certain things we have to talk about.' She spoke most solemnly.

The television grew louder, it seemed. They were on a ship, in the film, the man and the woman who would kiss at the end, holding on to the rail, staring ahead, talking to the sea. It was near the end. Maureen could feel the music preparing itself for the final sweep which would bring a lump to her throat, she knew it and dreaded it. Though her attention had been desultory, she knew that she wanted the woman to be happy for ever as she would be with that man. Something in her expression had hooked Maureen's interest; she knew that she would cry.

What a time to cry!

'Was that Annie?' Josh asked.

'Was it?'

'Listen.' He got up and went to the television, turned it down; waited. 'No. It must have been the wind in the chimney. Funny the sounds that makes. Do you want this up again?'

She would have said no, but he had already begun turning it up as he had asked the question and to her own confusion she did not stop it because she wanted to see the ending. Though she knew what happened. Even if she had not seen it before, she could have guessed, easily. Those impeccably virtuous people would have to clinch.

'You fuss about that child far too much.'

He did not reply.

Maureen was already exasperated. Other times, other impossibly empty times when he would not be goaded, came back to her. It was strange that she could feel so much impatience with him, so much ordinary peevishness in the middle of an attempt to begin to do something which would alter their entire lives.

The film drew to its close. The theme tune grew insistent and they kissed. She could not bear to look. There it was—the lump in her throat. Angry with herself, she got up and went to turn it off. The final chord was held and the picture showed a seagull suspended in the air, drifting on the currents in the sky.

She turned it off, beating the final note; in some minute way spiting that inconsequential, stupid part of herself.

'I'll have tea,' said Josh, still bent over that toy.

'Get it yourself then!'

'OK.'

She could have stamped her foot or thrown something at him. She went into the back-kitchen and made a pot of tea.

It was so hopeless! She could never even begin to tell him about it. He did not seem to realize that anything was going on.

She could get no response from him to help her achieve the necessary tension.

Maureen held the tray firmly and marched back into the room. The man was still there before the fire, every particle of him devoted to the red wheels and the yellow truck. She banged the tray on the table.

'Blister wants to collect me tomorrow night,' she said, and was instantly afraid of her rashness. Josh made no reply; she poured out a cup of tea and slopped a little, her hand was not quite steady. 'He's going to a dance with Beth and Jack and them and he wants me to go.'

'Do you want to?'

Now it was Maureen who paused. At first merely to get from a dramatic silence the respect which *his* silences drew to *him*. Then, in the quiet, the simple question sank swiftly and deeply to the bottom of her mind. Whatever answer she gave was bound to describe her love for Josh: and she did not know how to, or whether she wanted to or whether she ought to.

'Yes,' she said. 'I haven't been to a dance for months.'

She tensed her head slightly, as if flinching from a blow, but no blow came; then she walked aggressively towards him; it seemed the cup and saucer was merely an excuse.

'Thank you.' He set it down beside him. Sometimes he would forget that he had been given a cup and let it go cold. Ignore it, having accepted it; Maureen could not understand that.

She sat down and waited.

'Where is this dance?'

'Rosewain.'

'I've been to dances there.'

'I was thinking of stopping the night in Thurston so as not to be back late and disturb you and Annie. Blister could bring me up in the morning when he comes to work.' He would not say anything, she would have to do it all herself. She sipped at the tea and then drew a deep breath. 'Blister's—he's a scream!—me and him have some great laughs.'

'You should have him round here some night,' said Josh.

'I might. Yes.'

'That should do the trick.' He folded his knife and examined the renovated truck. Then he put it on the floor and pushed it towards Maureen: she lifted her legs and it bumped into the chair. Josh looked at her and smiled. Such a nice, sweet, gentle, loving open smile, she thought; like the man in the film—nothing to hide, always to be trusted. Once more the lump came to her throat.

'She'll like that,' said Josh. He got to his feet. 'I'm off to see how that beast is.'

'What?'

'The one I said had that bad cough. Vet said she needed medicine last thing at night.'

'Why can't Norman do it? Or Wilson? I said you worked too hard. It would be no trouble for them.'

'It's no trouble for me. I like nursing them.'

He took his cap and at the door put on his wellingtons.

'Don't wait up. I might take time.'

'You *always* find something to do when I want to talk.'

'Would you like a touch more coal on that fire?'

'No.'

He nodded and left her. Through the open door she had a glimpse of the black night and she shivered. There were times when she was afraid to be left alone. Josh would not understand that.

She was asleep in her chair when he got back. He looked at her for a while and on his face still was the strain and grief the old clergyman had seen. He stared at her for a while, helplessly.

Leaving her undisturbed, he went up the stairs and into Annie's room which he had painted himself. In strong primary colours, there were animals everywhere—awkwardly painted but vivid and happy—rabbits, chickens, lambs, donkeys, puppies, kittens, the whole room seemed to snuggle itself round the little girl. She lay on her back, arms thrown back over her shoulders so that her tiny hands nudged her small, sweet ears. Her breathing was light and regular, her breath and the smell of her swept into him and he stood above her unmoving as he had stood above her mother, lightening his own breath and matching its rhythm to hers.

Maureen woke up, saw the time and made for the stairs.

After a few steps, she faltered.

'Josh?' she whispered. 'Josh? Are you there? Is that you up there?'

He did not answer. In the gripped silence of the house he heard the hesitation in her breath and clearly sensed the fear.

'Josh? Josh?'

He went to Annie's door and looked down at her. Her back was to him; she was about to return into the kitchen.

'Maureen?'

She gasped and, turning fearfully, slipped a stair, bumped herself.

'What do you mean by frightening me like that?'

'Ssshhh! You'll wake her.'

'We've got to talk, Josh. We have to talk. And I *am* going out with Blister and Beth and them tomorrow night—you understand that?'

'Not so loud.'

It was said gently and she complied. She decided to wash the cups instead of leaving them for the morning as she usually did.

Cedric had soon found a place in the village; not quite the same but as yet not so apparently different either. He drank a little more than he used to and there were stories of the merchant navy as well as the Army. They were the same stories because his listeners wanted to hear the same thing; that was his conclusion and he expressed his contempt by lying his head off. The whore of Singapore.

A good day's work—mending that motor-bike and getting up to date on Maureen's carryings-on. And a good omen in the pub; Calthwaite had let his dog in, Duke, because he had bet that the dog would recognize the man who had hurt it, would remember after all these years. The dog had not remembered. Cedric felt as if he had been cleared of a false charge.

He was not so old as to let himself get out of condition. He did his knee-bends and a dozen push-ups; in the bedroom still, though the rest of the house was free.

CHAPTER THIRTEEN

SITTING contentedly in The Lion and Lamb playing Fives and Threes, Blister pretended to himself that he wished that Maureen had never been born. He would be quite happy, he told himself, to stay with the lads playing dominoes, having a few pints, no worries about what was what. He knew he was late and had stopped glancing up at the clock. There were only the four of them in the small snug and the dim wall light gave the group a feeling of closeness which Blister was enjoying, particularly on this night. The point was arriving where he would have to make the big decision about Maureen and take the action and the closer it came the more sensible he grew of the advantages his freebooting habits gave him. The other players were men he'd known all his life; two of them had been with him when he had been sent to prison for three months; they had poached together and gone thieving a bit, nothing serious, locally directed and on the whole tolerated locally for the scandalous gossip provided, and perhaps for fear of worse. In their late twenties their heroes were fighters and sportsmen and successful gamblers; himself the only one in anything smacking of regular employment—and that up at Ullaby Quarry which made it even harder to bear because people might think he'd gone there to please Maureen whereas it was no more than a coincidence. His staying on, though, was more than that; he had wanted to see Maureen by day as well as night.

That was the difference. It was this need to see her daily and as often as possible which distinguished her from the others he had gone with. The compulsion was not admitted to anyone;

certainly not to these friends who brooded over their dominoes in the warm gloom of the snug, as thriftily as they sipped the pints of mild. As they were playing among themselves and paying for their own drinks this pub-bare first day of the week, they took the cheapest beer, which they licked as if it were brandy, and played for a penny a shuffle. He kept her out of their lives. Nor did he allow Maureen to become confident of his devotion, he thought; and such a trick as this—keeping her waiting to be picked up for the dance—was part of an erratic but obstinate intention to let her see that he was not tied to her apron strings.

It would be their first full night together. It was all arranged. They would sleep on the leatherette settee in Beth's house. She had brought it with her from her parents' place because, in the first few weeks in the new council house, she and Jack had found it difficult to sleep and blamed it on the new bed which was not truly broken in; the put-you-up had been called into the breach and stayed as a proud guest-bed. Beth and Jack had no children, could not have any.

He concentrated on the game but he could no more let Maureen down than injure his own notion of his pride. As the dominoes tapped on the wooden board, he saw her, in her kitchen, waiting and, wanting her, felt deeply stirred, stung with slow charging contentment, that he would have her for the night, the full night; she would have left Josh; without question she would be his.

Her case was beside the door. It was rather big for just the one night but it was the only case she had. It was prominent, placed there, a presence in the room. Josh was in the old leather armchair, his hands locked behind his head, gently rocking it as he stared into the low fire, his stockinged feet thrust on the fender, threatening to be caught and burnt by any unexpected flame.

The television was off. No clock ticked. No cars passed. No neighbouring sounds. Only the suck of the fire.

Maureen was mending a pair of Anne's tights and the small navy blue woollen legs dangled limply from her lap as she bent over to concentrate on darning the big hole which had long ago appeared in the bottom and been allowed to grow unchecked until now. The silence was perturbing her, but switching on the television would make it more difficult to leave when the time came. She concentrated on her work; she was good at it, neat and efficient with a needle, and this small job made her feel less guilty about leaving Josh.

She still refused to tell herself that she was going to sleep all night with Blister. She knew it would happen, she was excited by it as she had been since Beth had suggested it. The whole thing sometimes appeared as an adventure, no different, really, from those times in the bedroom at her mother's, or in the fields between Thurston and Ullaby.

But there was something very serious about spending the night away from her sleeping child, her harmless baby, and this unsuspicious man with whom she had sworn to live to death, and the awareness of that beat against her concentrated calm as the sudden crackle of a knot of wood in the fire leapt against the silence and made her start. The needle had pricked her thumb. She watched the blood come out slowly but persistently, so dark this blood and strange when you stared at it and knew it was yourself. She let it gather and then licked it, disguising that movement by pretending she was covering a yawn. She did not want Josh to see the blood, did not want him to have any chance of connecting with her; and the yawn was not wholly false. She was growing tired in this silent attendance.

Perhaps he would not come. For a few seconds the anxiety was a real one and she was reinforced in her decision to go from Josh. Yet immediately following the resolution was relief at the prospect of there being no break with Josh, and an awareness of the harm that could then be avoided for Anne. Always she was tossed between fear of the loss and apprehension of the gain. Anne came late in her thoughts—she was so much more Josh's child than her own, she felt, and somehow that made it easier for her to excuse herself. It was all to fill in time, this worrying, she had gone too far to be able to turn back.

She was dressed to please Blister. Since her marriage she had bought few new clothes, but careful tailoring of her old outfits and discriminating buying at a discount from the shop in which she had worked gave her sufficient range. She was no longer the slim teenager whom unfriendly critics could well have called skinny and knowing elders cast in that type which was briefly clear but quickly smudged; she had thickened becomingly, her breasts were heavier but still supple, her shoulders fuller, her walk more relaxed, especially since meeting Blister, aware of the hope behind the whistles and the stares and prepared to spice it; perhaps because of the fell air, certainly because of her lazy life, her complexion was finer than ever it had been and the skin drew on the fingers to stroke it. Josh's care for her, his flawless love for her and the ease she had in that, had secured a foundation of easy growth into loveliness which this later passion for Blister quickened into real beauty.

She was very conscious of the erotic intention of her clothes and the hair so thoroughly washed and combed back, patiently dried with the small machine Josh had given her one Christmas. In that labourer's cottage she had spent the entire day preparing herself scrupulously; in that stone-flagged kitchen where not so long ago swollen ankles had chafed against the hardness of clogs, she had bathed and scented herself; from that most ordinary little place she would emerge dazzling. Before Josh, she was embarrased by this richness.

If only they were not married.

She finished her work on the tights and wanted to ask the time. Her own watch had broken and the clock had stopped. Josh had a pocket watch the vicar had given him; a large silver watch in a heavy case which bulged inside his breast pocket and had never lost more than a couple of minutes all the time he'd possessed it.

She hesitated and then decided not to ask him, telling herself she did not want to disturb him, quelling the rise of fear at the thought of engaging him.

It was strange, this time between them so silent: they might have been waiting the arrival of old friends.

Anne took her teddy under the blankets so that no one else would hear them talk. She squatted with her back straight so that the sheets and blankets draped around her like a miniature bell-tent, and there was space to sit her teddy in front of her. Her voice was silvery, and she spoke in sweet admonishment.

'You're a naughty teddy not being asleep. Mammy'll send a crocodile to eat you up and then you'll have no more babies. No. I'll sing you a song. Pretend I'm a daddy will you? Will you just pretend I'm a daddy and I'll sing you a song?

"*Baa baa, black sheep*
Have you any wool?
Yessir Yessir,
Three bags full.
One for the master,
One for the dame,
One for the lickle boy
That cries in the lane."

Oh. Are you still not asleep, teddy? Here's a kiss to take to sleep with you. There! There! One on the ears and one on the eyes and one on the nose. There!

'Now pretend I'm a mammy again. Yes? What have you been doing today? It's time to wash your face. Here's the cloth, here's the soap. Wash all round it. "Mammy! Mammy! The soap's got in my eyes." Don't rub. Silly teddy. "Mammy! Mammy! I can't see." Silly Teddy, find a cloth, rub with that. What a silly thing to do. Go to daddy for a kiss.

'Now pretend I'm a daddy again. All right? There, there.'

Josh had come up so quietly that even the sensitive hearing of the child had not been disturbed. For a few moments he had stood listening but only for a very short time: her chatter was too intimate; even though she was speaking to a doll he felt guilty for intruding.

He made a slight noise so that she would know he was there and be prepared for him.

'Daddy?'

'Yes?'

'*Really* Daddy?'

'Yes.'

A sort of rippling giggle scurried from under the sheets and the small bell-tent collapsed as the child dived for the unnecessary safety of pretended sleep. Josh put his hands gently around the small body, himself also moving under a pretence—that she needed his help to straighten herself out.

'Hello Daddy! You waked me up.'

'Fibber,' he replied, a most tender reproof.

'Can it be a joke I said?' She sat up; the light from the landing at once illuminated and deepened her wide eyes.

'Yes.'

'Well. I wasn't *really* asleep.'

'You should be. All little girls are asleep now.'

'Do all lickle girls have teddies to sleep with?'

'Some do.'

'Will you tell me a story?'

'It's too late for stories.'

'Just Snow White. Please. Please.'

She put her small arms around his neck and pressed her sweet-smelling face against his. Her fingers locked and she clung so that he had to bend down even further and sit on the bed; the alternative was to break her grip which he never liked to do.

'Please, Daddy.'

'All right. But then you'll sleep, won't you?'

'Yes.'

'Once upon a time . . .'

'Wait—Teddy wants to listen, don't you? There. He can hear now.'

'Once upon a time there was a King and a Queen and they lived in a big castle in the middle of a wood. One day they had a little girl and they called her Snow White . . .'

'And she was very beautiful, wasn't she?'

Downstairs it was with such confusion that Maureen heard her daughter and her husband that she could not be still. She got up from the chair and walked about the narrow kitchen. Why would he not come? She remembered when Blister had gone out with Beth—she had been reminded of that by her sister more than once—and how his habit of turning up late had signalled the end of that affair. But Beth had shouted at him; she would never shout.

Between the calm voice of the man near her, absorbed in her child, and the absence of the man she wanted and had made sacrifices for, she was stranded, and mingled with her irritation was self-pity.

It was Beth who was now holding up Blister. The plan had been for him to pick up Beth and Jack, drive to Ullaby, the four of them go for a drink and then on to a dance.

The longer he had played at the board the more tense and uncomfortable he had become. The image of Maureen had grown stronger and stronger in his mind's eye until his restlessness in the snug had matched hers in the cottage. Nobody had made him feel like that ever before.

But Beth was not ready. Jack suggested that he collect Maureen and come back for her but Beth was prepared for that and insisted that she would be ready in a few minutes. In front of Jack, and especially in front of Beth, there was face to be preserved and so Blister sat on the edge of the leatherette settee and smoked a little, soon dwindling into silence as Beth's pretence misfired and Jack's embarrassment made her anxious. She was flurried as she truly began to forget where things were. Finding her left shoe proved impossible. Eventually, Jack joined in the hunt with her and Blister watched both of them crawling over the carpet, sweeping their hands under chairs and other furniture. He made no attempt to help; it was all he could do to keep back his temper which, once flared, would scorch the entire evening.

Beth had always been a bit of a bitch, he thought.

At the bottom of the stairs Josh paused, partly to listen and make sure that Anne really *was* asleep, partly to gather his courage. Maureen was making no attempt now to disguise her impatience; indeed she found it difficult not to do something violent to express her disappointment.

'Why don't you not go?' Josh asked, steadily, looking directly at her as he moved across to his chair. 'It's late now, anyway.'

'What time *is* it?'

'After ten . . . By the time you've had a drink and got to Rosewain, it'll hardly be worth it.'

'They never get full until half past ten,' she said.

'I'd rather you didn't go, Maureen,' he said as he sat down, and though the tone was courteous and without any form of threat, the words were resolutely delivered. He looked tired now, but she saw instantly that he was set on a course, had finally taken up her challenge.

She did not want it to happen now. Not on this difficult evening when she was prepared for something else and was bearing the double burden of disappointed expectation and of guilt. It was too late now. Inside her head it was as if the protestations squirmed like living tormentors; she did not look at him but gazed at the fire, her cheeks burning.

Josh waited for a reaction, not unnerved by the silence.

'There doesn't seem much point in arguing anyway,' she replied, eventually. 'It looks as if they've forgotten all about it. Cup of tea?' She sucked the blood from her finger.

'No. Wait.' He clasped his hands in front of him and the tension which he thrust into his body seemed to ease his mind. 'Please. Maureen—don't look away. Please. Come on. Don't look away. I'll not say anything to hurt you. I just want to look at you when I say it.'

'Oh for Christ's sake, Josh, get it out!'

'I'm sorry to take so long over it.'

'So you should be. Tea?'

'That can wait.' He paused only slightly and again his voice was resolute. 'Annie and me love you very much, Maureen. That's what you've got to remember. We both of us want you to keep living with us. I'm not much of a dancing partner, I know that, and you must go out to enjoy yourself—but we love you and there you are. We always will. You have to know that.'

'I do know that! What d'you want to say *that* for? I feel the same way, don't I? Why are you so worked up about it? I'll make you some tea.'

She went into the back kitchen but could not repress herself.

'Just because I decide to go out for a dance with my own sister and her husband and a friend. They haven't even turned up! That's just like you. I'm stuck in this dead-end and the one night I get a chance to get out of it you throw a fit!' She was trembling in her anger and remorse—for his tone had stabbed her—and she banged around the little kitchen wanting to smash everything in it. 'What if I *do* want to go out somewhere on my own sometimes? I can't be expected to sit and stitch tights in here every damned night there is. Nobody can be expected to do that nowadays—not when you can do so much else!'

He did not say 'Whenever I've suggested going anywhere lately you refuse'; he did not contradict her complaint of isolation by instancing the number of times she was away from the cottage; he never reproved her, or so rarely and slightly as to be a switch which encouraged rather than the lash which deterred. But she said these things for him, to herself, in her own head, and was more vehement in response to her self-reproaches than she would have been to his. That was the trouble with Josh—you could never get anything going! Even this night, this so-called argument; he would just sit there and say his piece, then clam up.

And he was always Right.

It was that which skewered her until she squirmed. As far as she could remember, on every issue, Josh had been Right. He was so far above her as, at times, to be as distant as the garish plaster saints his looks sometimes reminded her of. He never pressed, never forced, never bullied nor shouted nor tormented. At times she was in awe of this rightness of his and at times she despaired of it: either way it took her out of the ordinary mixture of self she had rediscovered with such relief with Blister. Though Blister was not a quarter the man Josh was—in any way. Moreover, she vaguely recognized that her own growth into such a beauty, the intense tranquillity she occasionally experienced, even the fact that she had the strength to practise her deceit with such ease, came from the enhancement of her better qualities throu h proximity to one whose virtues appeared unshakeable.

She came back in with the tray and he smiled at her gently, unaccusingly, even a touch of merriment in the smile.

'All right, I'll stay,' she said, and as she said it she felt herself loving him very much.

Then the car would not start. Blister said nothing but Beth was clearly made to feel that her pantomime about getting ready was a direct cause of the engine failure. Jack, too, was nervous as Blister pulled and pulled on the starter and then leapt out, throwing up the bonnet with such violence that it was all but flung off its hinges.

Jack got out to show willing, Beth huddled on the cold front seat. Perhaps to make amends, she used a cupped palm as an ashtray.

Blister rapidly saw what had to be done.

'I'll need some light,' he said. 'We'll give her a push up to there.'

They heaved the car and it trundled up to a street lamp. Beth made no attempt to get out, resenting the injustice of the unspoken accusation.

'Shit this for a lark,' she said, after Blister had been unsuccessfuly occupied for about a quarter of an hour. 'I'm off back in.'

Jack tried to warn her by looks and attitude that this would be taken badly by Blister, but he had no effect on his wife who by now was unafraid of Blister, would have welcomed a fight.

In her sitting-room she put on one bar of the electric fire and flicked through a magazine, sitting, almost squatting, on the edge of the chair, in readiness.

They were in bed and they had made love. It was some time since they had made love so sweetly and they lay side by side holding hands, looking at the ceiling which was faintly stroked by moonlight.

The car had no respect for the sleeping village and roared through it, stopping outside Josh's cottage emphatically, marking the spot as clearly as if a small bomb had gone off there.

It was Beth who came and knocked on the door and Maureen was out of bed instantly to be down to open it to her.

Knowing he would complicate it unbearably for his wife, Josh stayed where he was and tried to ignore the whispering which drifted up the narrow staircase. It was not an easy decision. He remembered what the vicar had said about the man giving a lead—he had thought on that all the previous evening; it was just such a guideline he had hoped for from the old man even though, at the time, he had affected to contradict it. But it was no good forcing her to stay if she did not want to—was it?

He was *aware* of rumours about Maureen and Blister but so far he had been able to block them in his mind by relying entirely on the belief that she would tell him anything he needed to know on such a subject.

They had just made love and he trusted to that.

Maureen came back to the bedroom.

'Would you think I was really awful if I went?' Already she had the dressing-gown off and was pulling on her tights. 'It's only just after eleven and these dances don't warm up until half past. Their car broke down! Our Beth says that Jack nearly ruined his jacket helping to put it right!' Rapidly, rapidly, she dressed. 'It's ridiculous really, isn't it? The way these blooming motor cars play you about. You would think with all their modern inventions they could stop a car from breaking down. Did you see my . . . ? There it is.' She slipped on her dress and wriggled into it excitedly. 'Now remember! The cornflakes are in the bottom cage in the larder and the eggs are on the window-sill. She likes plenty of breakfast even though she tries to play about with it so see that she eats it all up.' Now she was dressed exactly as she had been an hour before: but in the new mood, she looked for something extra. She pulled open a drawer and discovered the hair-piece she had worn the very first time she and Josh had met. 'I'll take that with me just in case,' she said, daring herself to conquer the memory. 'I can always put it on in the car. Pins, pins—yes. Well!' She did not ask him how she looked but the twirl she did spoke that question. She darted at him and kissed his cheek and was away at the door quickly. 'Ssshh! I'll just go and give Annie a kiss and tuck her in. Remember what I said about the eggs.'

She left. He waited until the front door had gently closed, until the car had misfired several times and then departed, until its sound was all gone. Then he got up and after a glance at the place where they had made love, he went down to the kitchen and sat before the fire all night, feeding the low flames.

CHAPTER FOURTEEN

MAUREEN was late. It had been arranged that she would pick up Anne at Mrs Wilson's but it was the afternoon, not the morning, which saw her arrival there. She had not rushed. Blister had taken the morning off work and insisted on driving her to Ullaby, though Maureen would have preferred the less ostentatious transport of the bus. But he wanted them to be seen together.

'She's asleep,' said Mrs Wilson, by way of a greeting and added, 'poor thing. You'd better come in.'

The invitation was grudged. Mrs Wilson rarely had other women in her house.

'I can't stay,' Maureen assured her, but the spare old woman with straggling grey hairs on her chin ignored her and led the way to the kitchen. Anne was lying on the horsehair sofa in a white dress.

'What did he want to put that dress on her for?' Maureen used her real vexation as a spur to urge herself out of the silence. 'It'll be filthy in no time.'

'I expect he did what he could,' replied the pious woman, promptly. 'Men can't be expected to know the ins and outs of matters such as that.'

'Everybody knows that white gets dirty. Men *and* women—there's nothing special about *that*, Mrs Wilson.'

She used the woman's name to keep her at a distance and physically increased the distance between them by walking across to the child. She noticed the shiny coarseness of the covering on the sofa as she bent to scoop up her sleeping daughter and took care not to scrape her hand on it.

'You can leave her if you've a mind,' said Mrs Wilson, annoyed that her undoubted moral superiority and patent moral disapproval appeared to affect the young woman so lightly. 'I don't mind looking after her. She's a joy to me. Mr Wilson and myself are always pleased to see *her* coming along with her happy face—the image of Josh and like him in all her little ways, too.'

'They say she's got some of my features,' Maureen replied, stung by the exclusion.

'Do they?' Mrs Wilson moved across to her, swiftly. 'I can't see it myself. Maybe a little bit the nose, but the nose is nothing to go by in children, is it? It never turns out as you'd expect and even so, as I remember Josh, *his* nose was rather like that.'

'How do you know?' There was a pause, 'I mean—you didn't meet him until he'd left school, did you?' Maureen enjoyed that brief triumph, 'I should've thought people's noses would be set by *then*.'

Mrs Wilson sniffed as if to say 'Speak for yourself'.

'Annie,' Maureen whispered, rocking the tiny shoulder gently, 'Annie, wake up darling: Annie.'

'She looks tired out,' said Mrs Wilson.

'Annie.' The child stirred.

'She had every scrap of her dinner. Josh is always telling me she's a poor eater but she ate every morsel of what *I* put in front of her.'

'Mammy!' The voice was clear, welcoming, delighted. Maureen crushed the little girl in her arms and hugged her passionately.

'You'd think you'd been away for a six-month.'

The remark was useful: it stemmed the tears which threatened to overwhelm the mother and she brushed her eyes quickly on her daughter's shoulder.

'Did you bring me a present?' Anne asked, with sly daring, presuming on that hug.

'Yes,' Maureen lied. She would buy sweets later at the shop.

'Goody, goody, goody!' The child clapped her hands. 'Oh—I love you Mammy.'

This time it was the child who wrapped her arms around

the mother's neck. Maureen took advantage of the grip to stand up and so lift Anne with her.

'She'll want her coat,' said Mrs Wilson, making no move.

'I'll just put it over her shoulders. It isn't *that* cold. Is it in the back-kitchen?'

The implication that Maureen might actually go and look out the coat herself, invade the house, jarred Mrs Wilson to action. After the presentation of an apple in return for a peck from the child, she let them go.

As she walked back to her house, Maureen in her mind exaggerated the joust with Mrs Wilson to make it appear as a victory, needing confidence to face Josh when somehow the situation had to be resolved. Blister was no longer prepared to be discreet nor inclined to be considerate. The night had been seized by him to demonstrate the force of his want of her; the response her excitement had returned assured him of her real feelings. It was bad luck on Josh, he conceded hypocritically; but the thought of *him* having *her* another night . . . no.

Norman was standing outside her door as she arrived, sweating slightly from the weight of Annie but still insisting on carrying her, indulging the little girl's pleasure in this unexpected mothering.

'I was wondering,' he began, after various nods to her and grins to Anne who reached out and attempted to grab the neb of his cap, 'we were wondering if you'd seen Josh, that is, me and Wilson. If you'd seen him.'

'No. Why?'

'Well,' Norman took off the cap and scratched himself awkwardly. Both he and Wilson had sensed a connection between Josh's disappearance and Maureen's behaviour and it was difficult to confront her without revealing that. 'Last either of us saw him was about just after ten o'clock. We thought he'd come back here for his dinner with you, see? Anyway, time's getting on now and he still hasn't turned up.'

'He wasn't in when I went in to leave my case,' Maureen replied. 'Let's see if he's there now,' she suggested.

They went in. Smiling at Norman, Maureen went upstairs

She had unpacked her clothes and put the suitcase on top of the wardrobe earlier. Then she had been so charged with the effort to digest the previous night before encountering Anne and Josh that the place had had little effect on her. Now she stood a while, listening to the babble of Norman and Annie below; and the empty bed, the flowered wallpaper, the cold slate light through the window, the suitcase neatly shoved back into place—all of it made her sensitive to the abyss between her past and her future. What *was* she to do? How stupid, that careless yielding to Blister those months ago. She remembered the lurch inside her when she realized that she would do it if Blister asked her to; it had been as if she were too tired to resist. Exhausted by the unwanted complications of abstinence. And things were so easy with Blister; she felt, then, as she still did to some extent, that she could control Blister.

Most of all—that strain of for ever falling short of an unwanted idealized position was gone. Blister was ordinary—that was such a relief; and she enjoyed the uncertainties—the tension and dangers of her childhood were attractive once more; being so long abandoned they appeared enticing, full of adventure.

By such deliberate assessment did she try to account for her position and to justify it.

Yet it was all done outside the fact of Josh's love for her. In this bedroom they had slept side by side. He had not changed. She could not truthfully admit that she had ceased to love him. The gap between what she was with him and what she was with Blister took her through dark ways. She needed times like this to remember, to think, to rest and breathe.

It was at that moment, she would later say, that she first got the feeling that something terrible would happen. There, alone, in that chill familiar room. Perhaps the point had been reached, in that balancing of possibilities, which tipped the scales irretrievably against a past which glowed the more brightly the more decisively she left it. Not for years, she later said, had she felt forced to pray, as now she did; on her knees beside the bed, hurriedly whispering Hail Mary, Full of Grace . . . her eyes squeezed tight shut so that they hurt.

When Cedric found out about Josh's disappearance, it was

evening. He had half-expected it after their last talk. He was glad that he had not yet been found because he *had* to be the one who could unearth him; he ought to have been told much sooner, though, he thought, and shouted at Norman for bringing the news so late. Others might have discovered him by accident, he said.

But no one was looking, Norman replied. Wilson had concluded that Josh had strayed off on some legitimate business—helping an acquaintance perhaps, and in that action being carried off to another village to fulfil the obligation; something of that nature. And Norman's own worry, he intimated, was more the natural concern of someone who missed the mate he was supposed to be working with. He had been looking forward to having a talk with Josh as they were to work together through the afternoon. True, Maureen was very anxious.

That sentence settled the gravity of the situation as far as Cedric was concerned. He went up the village like a warrior sent from another country to bring hope to the beleaguered and assured Maureen that if anybody could find Josh, he could.

He borrowed Josh's motor-bike. As he wheeled it out, Blister arrived in his car; usually he stopped some distance away and pressed the horn. This evening he drove right up to the front door and got out. Cedric watched all this while starting the engine. Blister felt the intensity of the curiosity and returned a very hard look which acted on Cedric like the press of an accelerator and he set off.

Blister had come to tell Maureen that he had seen Josh on the lower slope of the fell, looking down at the quarry throughout the afternoon. In time, all the men had noticed him—the news would be round the village in a few minutes when they got back home. Not doing any work, not responding to shouts or to waves, just sitting gazing down or wandering a little way, apparently idly.

'Does that mean you've told him what's what?' he asked.

'No. I haven't seen him.' She wished Anne were not so quick: she could see the child looking from face to face with a disturbingly discerning expression.

'Well he must've worked it out for himself. Just as well. Right. Are we packed?'

'I can't go without telling him, Blister.'

'The arrangement was for me to pick you up here, packed.'

'I never agreed to that. I said I'd have to see what happened.'

'There's no need. It was *me* he was looking at up there. I'm glad it's out. Now then. Can I help you to pack up? You can sort out all the big stuff later.'

His impatience annoyed her. It was one thing to enjoy coarse treatment as from a lover; quite another to be bullied by a tense boyfriend. Called on thus roughly to abandon it, the small cottage, in which she'd been corked so tight she'd feared suffocation, now seemed a safe place; room enough.

'It's him or me!'

'Blister, please.' She looked at Anne.

'Him or me! You can't ask a man to hang around forever.'

He spoke hurriedly, as if he feared that Josh might rush in on him any moment and indeed he did glance at the door once or twice.

'I can't go without telling him.'

'Listen here. You don't come today—tonight—it's all over—finished—see? Nothing!'

'Blister, please. We can go outside to talk.'

'No more outsides for me, no. Me or him. Tonight. Now then. That's straight. Fair's fair.'

Maureen, her perception of these matters heightened, saw that Blister really was struggling to rise above his ugly and difficult temper. She recognized his cry 'Fair's fair' as being from one caught in her own dilemma—making an attempt to behave well despite the strain and the certain knowledge of ultimate failure. And it was fair, she thought, that he should be accorded the open or closed account he demanded. It *would* be a relief to settle it.

'What if I can't settle it in one night?' she asked.

'Maureen.' He spoke earnestly. 'If you don't know by now you never will. It's been months, not a day or two. I mean—the things you've said about how much—you know—us two—well you either meant them or you didn't. Now then.'

Annie's attention was by now riveted on Blister and she stood stiff before him, blinking up at his face, utterly concentrated.

'You've spoken your mind; that's fine. I'll talk it over to-night.'

'I'm not taking any bloody rubbish, understand?'

The swear word jarred Maureen sufficiently for Blister to react sharply; he saw that she flinched for Anne and was made aware of the child for the first time.

'I'll bring the car to the usual place about ten,' he said, by way of apology. 'About ten.'

Cedric was investing a great deal in his ability to find Josh. He went first along the paths they used to take on the training runs so many years ago and then he made for the villages nearby.

The pretence was in himself that he was conducting a systematic search: he would have proclaimed that he was sweeping along here and examining there and eliminating elsewhere—strategic doggerel from army days would have limped through the lips. But it would probably be as accurate to say that until dark he roared along on the bellowing machine like a man in a panic, directionless.

At lighting-up time he made back for Ullaby, intending to discover whether Josh had returned in his absence. He would not go to the house of course, nor would he ask anyone directly: there were ways in which he could elicit the information while maintaining his poise and its dignity.

He took the high fell-road back, the one which went past the quarry and it was here that he did have his hunch. He turned up the rutted tracks and roared on the inefficient machine, making for the small castellated building near the works.

He aimed the headlight directly at the door, and called out Josh's name—shouting it above the throb of the engine, hurling it at the stout little building. There was no reply but, he was later to boast, he could feel something. He knocked off the engine, put the light on battery, got out the large policeman's torch he had brought and which could serve as well for self-defence as illumination, and went into the place to find Josh sitting quietly on a pile of sacks, quite calm, it appeared.

'Hello, Cedric,' he said quietly. 'I thought it was you.'

'I knew you'd be here. I came straight here. When they

said you'd gone missing, I came straight here.' He did not trust himself to say more, was swollen with self-congratulation and pleasure to such an extent that it took him some time to recognize the degree of depression in his friend's voice and attitude.

He sat down beside Josh and played the torch's beam on the opposite wall.

'I knew you'd be here. I knew I'd be the one to find you.'

Maureen was particularly tender to Annie. She washed her in front of the fire and was constantly snuggling into her, licking her tummy to tickle her, pretending to nibble and bite on the pink flesh of the child. 'Mammy! Mammy! Mammy!'—the word peeled through the kitchen on many notes, tinkling into Maureen's ears, and she teased it out of her daughter again and again as if it were a charm she wanted repeated, one which she herself could not speak. 'Mammy, Mammy, Mammy.' The fair child gleamed with happiness, basking in what she took to be her mother's adoration.

Maureen would have needed more than simple charms to ward off the malevolent feelings of people in Ullaby that night; if sensations could have caught the elements, they would have beaten her door down, the blast and fury of them. Norman's increasing alarms about Josh's disappearance, mixed up with variously interpreted reports of the watch he had kept on Blister at the quarry that afternoon, set alight the keg of recrimination which rumours had fattened for months. Until now, though there had been much talk and much enjoyable malice, there had been no ferocity; too many had fallen in that village for people to be so upright. Births and marriages were registered in different ciphers on memory and in archive. Secrets had suppurated for years on end and bitterness was more likely to fester than to explode.

But she had gone too far. Out at a dance with another man and dressed like a young girl, shaking herself at him in the middle of the floor so that everybody stopped and stared at them so much that in the end even she had to stop and pretend she was embarrassed by it all. A full report of the dance was in every kitchen in Ullaby. Behaving as if she'd been let out of a women's prison (some wag said) after being put in for cannibalism—man-eating. The poor little girl to have to grow up with that sort of a mother around her neck! Dear God that Josh should have landed himself with rubbish like her. Oh! She'd been fine enough to start with—but then again, he'd spoiled her once that child was there, telling her she needn't do work, taking on other jobs himself to spare her the inconvenience. And she could be pleasant when she wanted—though she'd never taken up with anybody in the village—never really got in with anybody local. Still. No harm in privacy.

She should have *kept* her bloody self to herself! And such a man as Blister! Well. Like went to like in the end—whatever anybody said, dirt to dirt. Anybody who worked up at the quarry with him would tell you—nice enough fellow when he was quiet: never had much of a bait, mind, and you could tell he'd been dragged up by the way he'd no regard for his clothes or things like that, he wasn't to blame there: but when he turned! By God! And you could never tell when it would be.

Well he'd been in prison, hadn't he? No need to be half-hearted about saying it, he'd done his time of course and paid his penalty and what not, but it just showed you the type. There was no getting away from it.

It was clear now how she'd got Josh. Maybe he was a bit too lacking for his own good but a decent woman would have taken that into account, not just degraded herself in front of him. That's what must have happened. And he would think she was wonderful, of course, knowing no better.

When, much later, someone did knock on her door, the hammering was so loud that Maureen was frightened by it. She had spent a very agitated few hours, fluctuating between regret and resentment, guilt and yearning, being trapped in the place for want of someone to guard Anne. She had packed two cases, one for herself and one for the child, not, she had told herself, to ease a flight with Blister but in case of an emergency. She had also packed some of Josh's things in a carrier bag, acknowledging a possible apprehension about his disappearance which had no part in her chief concern which was how she was to react to what was undoubtedly a clear and decisive protest of his. Neither her solitude nor the urgency of the occasion itself had brought her to any clear conclusions about that, although there was one thing she held on to obstinately: she was perfectly happy with Blister and felt no strain. It wasn't only the sex part (though that *was* marvellous) but she was just more herself with him. Weighing how much that was worth against the worth of Josh was beyond her; she could find neither balance nor ratio.

So the knock was like the axing of a knot, the clanging of a bell the banging of a hammer—unmistakable prompt to action.

She had no chain-lock and so paused before opening and asked who it was. Hearing the vicar's voice she was at first irritated—that such a man as he should have caused her trepidation, and that he should interrupt such a personal matter—but then she was impressed; of all the people she knew, Josh would be more likely to confide in this peculiar priest than in any other. She opened the door to him and he came in, shaking off the rain as carelessly as a dog. He put his little fingers in his ears and pulled at them, trying, she supposed, to dry them or pop them, there was no way of telling. 'Well,' he began briskly, 'he's not strayed far, thanks be to God, and he's safe and sound. At the moment he is with Cedric Tyson and it's better that he stay there the night. It was Cedric found him near the quarry and he's had the most terrible job to persuade him to come down. However he did and all praise to the good Samaritan.' The vicar rubbed his hands and beamed at Maureen, who was sure the news was being filleted or fed her in easy stages. He shook off more raindrops and with that gesture he appeared to shrug out of one attitude and into another. 'You see he's a strange boy,' he said. 'People don't realize *how* strange he is because he makes great efforts and lives as he could be expected to. But his real concern is some kind of inner concern. Forgive my talking to you as if you were ignorant of him, my dear, I know he loved you far more than he's ever loved anyone else and so you must understand this much at least—but I have to begin where I can, beggars can't be choosers. I used to think, you know, when he was at the Home with me, I used to think if only he could do something wrong, even mischievous, even a little naughty. And that's what the trouble is here, you see. He's fastened himself on to his family—you and Anne—you two are the only world he has ever had. Any religious feeling, any family feeling, any liking for this place and the people in it —all tied itself up in you when you met. The difficulty is, I think, that people who make such absolute decisions forget the frailty of others. And in Josh's case there is some fearsome determination in him not to learn what might in any way harm what he values. Of course, what he values are what all we Christians value, that's why people like him and admire him and he *is* a real, a true Christian man; he could have been called on by Our Lord, I sometimes think in moments of sentimentality. But even the great values of the New Testament cannot be applied to life without the understanding that life might not live up to them.

'My dear, I see you are impatient: I talk too much. But I love him as I would love a son. And I watch over him as over a fragile soul. He does not want to see you yet—not tonight, anyway; and I suggest not tomorrow or even for a few days. He suggests you go to stay with your mother. You see, my dear, someone saw—forgive me but it would be cruel to leave you in ignorance—someone told him that last night you, shall I say, stayed with another man and he does not know what to say or do.'

CHAPTER FIFTEEN

CEDRIC had struck when Josh, weak from the repression, the wakefulness and the fear of the previous night, had been most stretched. The simple gossip—it was all around the district by mid-morning—had not been questioned and Cedric was careful to leave his friend alone with the news.

He had been dazed since then. All the ignored suspicions had been ignited and the shock was very great.

He wanted to be on his own, he'd explained to Cedric in the quarry building; and Cedric had suggested staying with him. The vicar had been waiting at Cedric's and insisted on talking to him despite Cedric's looks and hints. Josh had said very little, but welcomed the talk, helpful talk and full of words he recognized as being the touchstones of his thought—'love', 'understanding', 'duty', 'help', 'kind', 'family', 'work'. The vicar had seen his uncertainty and, guessing at the extent of the difficulty, he had fallen in with Cedric's plan that Josh should stay there.

Cedric gave him his mother's room. He had made some rudimentary changes in it since her death but though the more obvious signs of an old woman were hidden, the atmosphere was clammy with her presence. Josh would have preferred to sleep on the settee in the kitchen but Cedric insisted and he did not care to argue. The sheets were flannel and slightly damp. The window had been screwed shut because Mrs Tyson had feared night air. In that cheerless, unhappy place, the only colour was in the patchwork quilt; even there, browns greys, and bottle-greens dominated the pattern.

They had eaten bacon and eggs and fried bread and Cedric

had waited until Josh was in bed before washing up. It was arduous work for him in his impatience to scour the pans and see that all the grease was rinsed away, but he wanted things to be properly clean and neat for Josh. He had mentioned his impression of Maureen's housekeeping; so intoxicated by the turn of events that he could not recognize what would help or what hinder his own cause.

Josh was there! With him! He would look after him—they would see! He had learned to cook, he could keep things clean about a house, he wanted nothing better than to fend for this man. Then they would have times together! Talking about general subjects in the evenings; never having to go out and look for company; somebody to do things for. And maybe he would persuade Josh to take up running again, you never could tell; all in good time, of course; but he'd hunted out the schedules and they still applied.

When he had finished the washing-up he made two cups of Bovril and went to the bottom of the stairs, one in each hand, walking as if on a high wire across his own kitchen. Gently he called up the stairs, 'Josh, would you like a cup of Bovril, Josh? Josh?' And waited, but there was no reply.

He stood for some time, straining to create a response, thumbs whitening, pressed in the saucers. Then, 'I'll not bother you if you're asleep,' he said aloud, feeling pleased at his delicacy. For really he was ravenous for the man's company. Cedric was all but incapable of comprehending what his sly revelation had meant to Josh and what it might do to him. That Josh was under his roof now was an event of such importance that all other considerations were blotted out.

The fact that he did not, as yet, insist and that he did try to contain his excitement was like the wariness of a hunter who increases his efforts when given unexpected good luck and at first waits to reassess, lets the fullness of the new situation be appreciated, seeing a prize outside all normal expectation.

Cedric let himself out into the backyard; the house was too cramped for him. The rain was still quite heavy, thrown down from the clouds which swept raggedly and furiously across the sky. He stood there a few moments and then began to shadow-

box, taking care to keep quiet.
Anne, what would become of Anne?

When he thought of the child the tears would surge into his eyes and it was only the fear of incurring Cedric's presence and commiseration which would be prompted by hearing the sobs which checked him. Yet it was difficult to check himself. He was very near panic.

What would happen? Would they live apart? Would Maureen want to see him again? Maybe she was very unhappy in that cottage. Ought he to have lived in Thurston after all? How could he face her again, knowing that she had been with Blister and stayed with him and—He would not let himself imagine their two bodies.

Just as Maureen had been sharpened in certain ways through her life with Josh, so he also. Maureen had provided the living ideal of someone Beautiful, Loving, Warm, Homely, Friendly, Constant. It might not be too much to say that the idealization of a Christian image of himself had come out and fixed itself on her. She could do no wrong as far as Josh saw it. Sometimes, many times, he would be surprised at some of the things she said or bewildered by certain of her actions—her swearing, for example, or her malice towards the vicar or her short-temperedness with Anne, her high-handedness with Mrs Wilson—but those were insignificant pin-pricks and served only to awaken more powers of tenderness. He had never got over the fact that she came and lived with him, that she kissed him and made his meals, that she stayed with him and had his child, that she slept with him and made a home for him. The gifts he had received from her were endless and daily he appreciated them. He had to live up to her. He had to see that he was worthy of her. And so from being good to her, he became at first marvellous and then, through over-enthusiasm on his part and some resistance on hers—the two movements not synchronizing and the fault continuing like the slipping of a notch between two small cog-wheels which can eventually throw out an entire and massive system—he had toppled into undesired care, even extravagant thoughtfulness which had, for example, led him to fear for her physical comfort so deeply after the birth of the child, that he had been unable to make love to her without insistent reassurances being given.

Moreover, he misinterpreted clear signs in his idealized love. Her sexual coolness after the issue over contraceptives and so on was painful to him; he knew that she would not be so if she really loved him, he felt that she needed more caresses, more obvious loving, times out together, a new courtship—but he ignored that because in his blind, romantic idealization, her aloofness signified a kind of purity which is the perfect end of all idealizations. Being a mark of purity it was not only to be accepted, it was to be encouraged and savoured and fully understood. The mixture in him of two unselfconscious sets of characteristics—the one derived from nature which took things as it found them and the other from religion which found things as it wanted them—had been strengthening on its religious side ever since the marriage and that spiritual emphasis was given connection with his own childhood, in which it had been implanted, and with present circumstances through his daughter, whom he worshipped.

It was as if he were at his own ear whispering these questions to himself without a pause or a change. Eyes wide open, child-wide glaring at the black ceiling, like the ostrich egg which must be pecked open. But Cedric had completed the gradual work of the past months. Now Josh had to know for ever that the shell was broken; and even if it re-sealed itself, it could again be broken; that he had to come out, step outside the old comforts and certainty, and make of the change what he could.

He dozed a little and woke at dawn with a simple plan which had come in the light sleep. Something the vicar had said . . .

He loved her, that was all: if others loved her and she loved others—well, that was how it was. But he loved her whatever, and would live with her.

The break was healed. He had found the way and could again, as before, be certain.

Cedric heard him going down the stairs and was out of bed instantly. He grabbed the quilted yellow dressing-gown he took pride in and scudded down the stairs. Josh was fully dressed, even his cap was on, standing by the door.

'Sorry to wake you up, Cedric. I thought I'd been quiet.'

'No. It wasn't you. Yes. Well . . . What time is it?'

'I don't know. Can't be much after six.'

'I thought you didn't start at Wilson's till seven these days.'

'It's not Wilson's I'm headed for.' Josh was pleased with his decision; it solved everything, he thought. 'I'm off back home.'

'You can't do that.'

'What?'

'She's—not after what she's done. She's lowered herself. You can't want that.'

'It doesn't matter what she's done,' Josh spoke carefully, 'it's how *I* feel about it that counts.'

The cold kitchen was chill from dawn and only half-lit. The silence between them clenched Cedric's feeling hard.

'No,' he paused: then repeated, the tone more desperate, a hand reaching out to Josh. 'No. I won't let you. No. She's not good enough for you, Josh. You'll do yourself harm trying to get back what's lost. Let her go, Josh. She's showed she wants nothing to do with you. Stay here. I can look after you as well as she did.'

Josh listened as a polite guest listens to a host, giving him the benefit. Aware that he was not touching on the man's nerve, Cedric drove harder, hoping the disturbance of the previous day could be repeated.

'How do you know she wants you back? Like as not she'll have run away to him last night. I mean—she was pretty effing open about it, wasn't she? So for a start, on that side of it, what's likely to happen again is what's happened once. She's as good as said sod-you—hasn't she? Who could go back under those circumstances?'

'I don't care what's happened,' said Josh, dogged, scenting weary complication and the renewal of a struggle he had thought to be relieved from. 'She's my wife and that's that.'

'Ah—but is she? Is your wife the woman who leaves you and shames you with another man, eh? Is that a wife? Is a wife somebody who doesn't even keep your house clean for you when you don't even ask her to do any work? These things need to be taken into consideration. I would say she's less than a wife with what she did; only worth forgetting.'

'I must be away.'

'Wait. I'll walk back with you. Wait!'

Cedric left him to go up the stairs. He was trembling, switching from anger, against what he saw as Josh's stupid and pointless obstinacy, to panic that he might be abandoned.

He changed rapidly.

As soon as he came down the stairs, Josh opened the door and went out.

The village was deserted. None of the farms had started up and the only sounds came from birds, occasional shivering notes. Josh walked eagerly, and however Cedric tried to slow down the pace, he was unsuccessful. He could not bear to look at the younger man, whose expression was alight with expectation.

A few yards from his cottage, Josh stopped.

'Thanks for taking me in last night,' he said.

'What you mean is you don't want me to come any further with you.'

Josh nodded and went on, leaving Cedric blowing his hands, his breaths misty. However cold, he would wait to see what happened.

Maureen had been unable to resist Blister's demand that she leave with him. The vicar had frightened her, bringing out implications which she had deliberately tried to ignore; she *knew* about Josh's innocence and was made afraid by the reminder. She had persuaded herself that it would be useless to insist on seeing Josh when he had so plainly asked her not to; while the advice about going to stay overnight with her mother was something she hugged to herself as providing an excuse for a possible departure. Even now she thought concealments would somehow smuggle the facts through.

Her irritation and shame, her anxieties and indecisions had made her easy prey for Blister, whose demands were mercifully simple and could be met.

They passed the vicar on their way into Thurston. It was raining still and Blister slowed down to offer the old man a lift but Maureen urged him on and turned her head away as she passed by the old clergyman. Anne waved to him.

'I thought you would come back to your own hearth this morning and I wanted there to be a welcome for you,' the vicar said. 'You don't mind, I'm sure. The key was under the stone on the sill. I've only been here a few minutes—Hetherington gave me a lift up in his van, he's been working in with the police looking for these sheep-stealers. They must be local men, they think, taking them only in ones and twos. I put a fire on and made a pot of tea—it's still quite warm—have a cup.'

Josh was glad to see the vicar but walked across the the stairs at this first hiatus in the monologue.

'They're . . . I'm afraid they're not here. They're in Thurston. Here. Two spoonfuls, isn't it? Yes, they're in Thurston.'

Josh felt a lurch of dismay. Already by that simple act, it was more difficult. He had found this solution which was easy but it must not be delayed: it must be transmitted immediately when things were as they were now.

'I'll go down.'

'Hold on, Josh,' the voice was jocular, persuasive, just a touch over-emphatic. 'This is no time to go visiting. Honest people are in bed at this hour. You and I are the exceptions who prove the rule. Sit down a while and drink this tea. You look as if you could do with it.'

But Josh was reluctant. Apart from fearing the delay, he did not want to listen to the vicar for another hour or two. He had appreciated the previous evening's talk but he did not want any more.

'I'll go out for a bit,' he said.

'You want to be on your own, eh? I understand that. These things must be settled between a man and his solitary conscience. I understand that. If I were a better shepherd, Josh, I would ask you to go down on your knees with me at this time, to pray for guidance, but I've never been one for low-church gestures. In spirit I am on my knees, commending your life into the hands of Him who made us all that we might live His perfect grace to see. Remember the words of a psalm or some action of His and take heart from your insignificance. I talk too much for you—poor boy. You will have to talk yourself some day, even that sacrifice, Josh, you might be forced even to that to get her back. You love her very much, don't you? There, don't reply. Words would bring you to tears; I'll go. I cannot drive you from your own house; I must go. My prayers stay with you. Follow your own heart, Josh—it won't lead you in false ways.'

Cedric let the vicar come up to him, standing in the road, obliging him to stop.

'Are they all right in there? Do they want any help?'

'He's better left alone.'

'Not with her. She can twist him round her finger.'

'She isn't there.'

'I knew! I told him!'

The vicar took Cedric's arm, restraining him from rushing down to the cottage.

'He particularly asked to be alone.'

'He'll want to see me.'

'I think he has great difficulty knowing what he wants except this. At the moment he wishes to be alone. We who love him or like him must remember that.'

'Josh and me—we're like that!' Cedric jabbed out his right hand, the index and middle fingers crossed.

The vicar grasped the outstretched hand roughly and tightly.

'You must stay out of it. Whatever your feelings—you must not attempt to influence this affair.'

'He stayed with me. It was me he turned to. There's no argument over that. None. Let go!'

The last words were a cry; Cedric had seen Josh pushing his motor-bike out on to the road. A gun was jutting out of the side-car. The young man looked at the two of them and then kicked the starter, making no acknowledgement.

'Bloody let go of my arm!'

The vicar only gripped more firmly. Cedric pulled and heaved so hard that the old man was dragged, resisting, along behind him.

'Josh! Wait! You stupid effing old prat. Josh! Just a minute.

I'll come with you. I'll be quiet. Let bleeding go, you old bastard! Josh!' The name was lost in the sudden silence-ripping crash of the bike. Josh revved up quickly, and moved off.

Cedric hit out at the vicar, hit his narrow, bony arm several times with a chopping punch. But when the old man did let go, Josh was well away. He stood, breathing laboriously, rubbing the bruised arm with a rather shaking hand.

Cedric turned to him, his face twisted with frustration and anger.

'You,' he said, prodding the air between them with the index finger so lately crossed to represent friendship. 'You, Are an interferin' old sod.' The sound of the engine grew fainter and insults released in heat seemed inexcusable in this calmer time. 'That bein' a vicar. Be thankful for it. And being an old man. That's what's saving you.'

'*Your* love is so soon turned to hatred,' said the vicar, 'that I am glad to protect Josh from it. I thought you were a friend of his. But you merely want to dominate him; you want him to obey you in all things. I'm glad he was able to get away from you. I shall try to see that he stays away. You're a cruel man; you would hurt him as you've hurt me.'

'You try to turn him against me—now listen, vicar or no vicar, listen—you try to turn me and him against each other and watch out. Now remember!' Cedric jabbed at the clerical collar and the old man's head jerked back, abruptly. 'That won't save you, either.'

CHAPTER SIXTEEN

MAUREEN had been listening for his motor-bike since waking up. She anticipated his arrival with certainty.

The small kitchen was crowded. Blister stood beside the sink, stripped to his vest, shaving with great care. Jack was making large demands on the limited space by an open-armed reading of the *Daily Express*—the big pages held wide while his head bobbed around the print like a buoy on choppy water. Beth moved erratically between the cooker and the table, now with some bacon, now with fried bread, now with jam, now fresh tea—curlers bristling under the shadeless light. Anne sat at the corner of the table nearest the cooker, carefully trying to spread a lump of hard margarine on a slice of white, soft bread. Maureen held herself tightly against her present distaste and her imminent fears. She was so sure he would come that she listened as hard as she had ever listened for his bicycle bell in the days when he had courted her.

The wireless played pop music and all the talk was in the nature of shouting.

'We'll look after you, won't we?' Beth was addressing Anne who smiled gently up at her. 'Your Aunty Beth'll love to have you in the house—and your Uncle Jack as well—isn't that right? Jack? Yes—well—there'll be plenty for you to do. Plenty of people your age on *this* estate. Don't put your elbows on the table, there's a good girl. She suits blue, doesn't she?' Maureen nodded. 'I think your Aunty Beth might buy you a blue dress for your birthday. You know, one of those with lace up at the throat and round the wrist-ends—it'll look smashing on you.

Mind—you won't be able to mess *that* up by playing about with your breakfast. Let me spread it on for you—it'd drive a body crackers waiting for you to finish. There. Now eat it.'

'There's a man in Glasgow,' quoted Jack, 'who walked three miles on his hands for charity.' He looked up. 'Takes some doing that, you know.'

Anne lifted up her bread in her hand. Where Beth had pressed on the margarine, there were holes. Maureen had heard the bike draw up and stop and now she counted to herself, imagining Josh coming around to the back door. Blister stopped shaving only momentarily when he saw him. It was Beth who sang out 'Come in!' ('What else could I say?' she was to protest later, 'he would have come in anyway.')

The little girl slid off her seat, squeezed around the table on the side away from her mother (sensing the route might be barred there) and rushed against Josh who lifted her into his arms and hugged her dearly.

Only the wireless played—a coarse and raucous voice unintelligibly urging on a violently noisy group. It was Maureen who got up and turned it off. Beth had gone back to the cooker after the glare from Jack who kept to his paper, though regularly glancing at Blister who was taking extra care with the shaving of his chin.

'I've come to ask you to come back,' said Josh. He spoke directly at Maureen, ignoring the other three adults in the room. ('He could have said hello,' said Beth later, 'hello isn't asking too much.')

'She's staying here,' answered Blister. ('Just what I would have done myself,' Jack was to say. 'Bloody cheek—shoving his way in like that.')

'Maureen?' Josh spoke her name gently. 'Can we have a minute by ourselves together?'

'Anything you have to say, say in front of us!' Emboldened by Blister's surliness and her sister's silence, Beth took an initiative. 'You needn't think you'll get round her in private.'

'Shut up,' said Maureen, fiercely.

'Why should she?' Blister stared at Maureen's reflection in the mirror. 'She's talkin' sense.'

Josh held up Anne with one arm; the other hand he pressed

to his temples where a block of pressure was building up rapidly and threateningly.

'I just want to talk,' he said.

'We could go in the front room,' Maureen suggested.

'Oh no!' Blister put down the razor and turned around. 'I've had enough of this half and half business. You make up your mind. Him or me. We're both here. I respect him for coming for you but that's no reason to make you a present to him. It's up to you.'

In the silence, Anne, who had clung more and more tenaciously to Josh, began to whimper.

'You see!' Beth was indignant. 'Upsetting a little girl!'

'Beth—shut up!'

'Him or me.'

'That's fair,' said Jack. 'Couldn't be much fairer than that.'

'You must do what you want,' said Josh—still his gaze fixed on his wife. 'You needn't listen to this lot, you know. It's *you* that matters.'

'Now that's enough,' said Blister. 'She doesn't need any advice.'

The force in the front of his head was becoming painful. Josh wanted to put Annie down and give himself a rest but the little girl clung so hard.

'Please, Maureen,' he said, the words going further away from his mind, 'I want to live with you whatever happens.' ('He had no shame,' Beth subsequently reported. 'Standing there saying a thing like that at half past seven in the morning.')

'I'll have to think it over.' Maureen spoke in a clipped tone of voice—the sound of it, so hard and contained—a thousand miles from her feelings. It was the fear of appearing foolish which counted most strongly with her as Josh more and more urgently asked her to come back to him—the fear of everyone saying that she did not know her own mind, and was silly to cause all the trouble for nothing. If only Josh had not been so —straightforward, so blunt about it all; given her a chance by being less direct.

She could not answer yes or no.

'Yes or no!' Blister shouted. 'Give the man an answer. Yes or no.'

Josh turned to Blister for the first time and spoke very haltingly.

'You've no need to shout at everybody. It's not a thing to shout about—splitting up a family.'

'Oh no. Don't get at me.'

'Who else?'

'It takes two to tango.'

'Maureen. Annie and me would like you to come back with us.'

'What d'you mean, Annie and you? She stays here.'

'This isn't her house.'

'Kiddies stay with their mothers,' said Beth. 'Any git knows that.'

'Not with you lot.' Josh spoke simply. 'I wouldn't want her to be here with you.'

'Rotten bloody neck!'

'Beth! Shut up! Just keep your big fat mouth shut!'

'It's *my* house. I'll say what I like.'

'Josh. Give Annie back to me and we'll talk about it some other time.'

'No.'

'Blister? Are you going to let him get away with that?'

'Another word from you, Beth, and I'll murder you—honest to God I will. This is between Josh and me and Blister so keep your big nose out. Now that's the last time.'

'She's right,' said Jack.

'You'd suck anybody's bum for peace and quiet, you would.'

'That sort of language—that,' Josh shrugged. 'Children can't be brought up in that.'

'This was clean air till you came in with your farmyard shit, thank you very much.'

'I think,' Blister spoke firmly and authoritatively, as he understood it. 'I think he's right. She'll be better off in the place she knows, the kiddie, till it's all blown over. It'll be a lot handier for us two, anyway, Maureen, let's admit it.'

'Who'll look after her?' Beth demanded.

'Half of Ullaby'll be only too willing.' Maureen spoke bitterly. 'They'll love that. Our house'll be a mother's union in ten minutes. They all want to get their hands on Josh. But I'm not having it. That's flat. Now stop all this stupid talk and give me that child.'

The pressure in Josh's head was now severe and his hatred of three of the adults in the room could no longer be contained. He saw one course he could take and threw himself on it.

'No!' His loud voice, contrasting with all his previous utterances, checked them. 'No! She's mine. She's coming with me!' He raised his free arm, making a fist of the hand, and looked directly at Blister. 'Try to stop me—any of you—and we'll have trouble. NO!'

The last shout was as Maureen lunged across to grab Anne. Josh turned quickly to shield her and the child's head struck the door-frame. She began to scream. Josh's face shook with the strain and he pushed out at Beth who had come around the other way. The action was more violent than he would have intended and she fell back, bumping into Maureen and upsetting the table, knocking over the tea-pot which spilled over Jack.

Josh made for the door and as Maureen gathered herself to grab a second time, she felt her arms pinned to her side as Blister grabbed her.

'Let go! Let go!' She shouted in panic and in pain. 'Oh please, please, let go!'

'Oh what a bloody rotten mess this place is!' Beth shouted at Jack, using him as someone to blame. 'How the hell is a body expected to clean up this filth before work?'

'Please, Blister.' Maureen was sobbing now. 'Please. Please. NO!'

Josh had kicked the motor-bike into action and that set off Maureen once more.

'Get that squalling bloody female out of this sodding bloody kitchen!' Beth asserted her rights.

Crying heavily now, Maureen let Blister take her into the front room where they had spent the night.

'It's you can clean it all up,' Beth shouted after her. 'You're free all day.'

CHAPTER SEVENTEEN

Mrs Wilson took charge of the child through the day, saw that she was clean and gave her two hot meals. Norman, who had always liked the little girl greatly, made use of the situation to let loose all his avuncular generosity. As Maureen had predicted, there was no shortage of offers of help from the village. Even old Wilson himself was seen to chuck her chin and hoist her on the tractor seat with him for little rides. She looked well and happy and Josh told her that her mammy had gone away on holiday.

In the immediate short-term this was true. Blister quit his job at the quarry and took Maureen to Blackpool until the money ran out. She had wanted to come to say goodbye to Anne but he had threatened her and she herself accepted that, the break being made, it would be as well to have some time completely with Blister, to see if it worked between them *really*; time to assess the strength of her feeling for Josh and the balance between new pleasures and former satisfactions. She thought a few days away from the scene of it all would help to clarify matters. In some ways she felt she was being brave, meeting the situation so badly. She sent a postcard every day and often said that both Josh and Annie would be better off without her.

For when Blister had led her through into that front room, chill, bed unmade, curtains half-drawn, the radios and motors of the estate shuddering the workers into life, he had put his hand across her mouth and bent her backwards until she had been forced to collapse on the bed. His mouth, his hands, his drive, dictating that there be pleasure, that the tension be transformed through sex into excitement—that was what *she* wanted, wasn't it? Him ready to enter, herself made ready to receive him—that was *her* aim in life, wasn't it? The pleasure as he came in, the force of him and the opening to him—that was worth anything, wasn't it? And more, and more—wasn't it?

When Cedric fully realized that he was irrelevant to Josh's future, of negligible account in the emotional life of this man to whom he had offered everything—he was bitter indeed. No quarrel he had ever pursued had bred on such bitterness.

Thinking to gain from immediately previous goodwill, he challenged Josh directly—came down to a field where the younger man was working and called him down from the tractor. The gulls which had been circling above the machine now glided above the two men, light and dark, standing there in the exposed field which at one end climbed some way up the fellside.

'Where do I fit in then?' Cedric demanded, after scratching small-talk had encouraged nothing but signs of impatience from Josh. 'I come to see you—the bloody place is full of women and Norman and Wilson and other kids. I ask you out—it's no—"Annie this", "Annie that"—she'll dominate you if you're not careful, that kid. We were supposed to be mates.'

'We still are.'

'Prove it!'

'Cedric—I've this field to finish.'

'Prove it! Go on. We're supposed to be mates, I said: we are still, you said. Now I say—prove it!'

'You can't prove things like that.'

'You can!' In the desperate blindness of his need and his frustration, Cedric reached out with both hands, grabbed Josh's jacket lapels, tugged him and began to shake him. The words which had been looping through his mind for days now began to force their way out. 'Who do you think I am anyway? I could tell them one or two things about you. Effing blue-eyed boy! All take and no give. Effing traitor. You just used me—I'm just good enough when there's nobody else; when I came in last night even effing Norman gets more out of the conversation than I do and what sort of a mate is he? Go on! How much do you like him?'

'There's no need to go on about it, Cedric. I'm sorry if you feel a bit left out.'

'Do you like him better than me? You do! Don't you? Admit it!'

Josh put his hands on Cedric's to pull them away but the grip was too tight. Cedric was shouting, almost howling now, the words a meagre release for the store of pain. The intensity of it troubled Josh, who reacted by restraining his impulse to push Cedric away. The older man's grip, the thrust of his white, tense face, the smell and the pain of him became more oppressive each moment.

'Everybody likes Norman.'

'But everybody doesn't like Cedric! Eh? Effing admit it! Here's me thinking you're different. Here's me thinking you can appreciate things! Why didn't you take me with you to bring your little girl back? I would have helped. I could move in with you now. I could always be there—these rotten effing fly-by-nights say they'll help forever but they won't, you know. No. Not even for you. *I* will.'

'There isn't room.'

'There is.'

'I want Maureen to be free to come back home whenever she wants to. Now let me go, Cedric—you're just getting yourself worked up. I've this field to finish.'

Cedric pulled Josh tight towards him and glared. In that awkward, frantic look was an attempt to articulate the force of his feelings and communicate them as he had failed to do through language.

'Take all, give nothing!' He pushed Josh away. 'Take all, give nowt! You're a nobody, a nothing, you're all show, you're a traitor, an effing rotten traitor!'

Cedric backed away as he shouted these insults and then bit his wrist to establish a contact between the counterstraining parts of himself.

'It's finished! Over! Over! Over! Give nothing!'

He turned and left Josh. It was not until he was almost out

of the long field that he heard the engine start up. So Josh must have watched him walk all the way.

He was not sure what he wanted, but, unable to stay in Ullaby, he had walked down to Thurston and eventually discovered himself to be searching out Blister perhaps as an ally.

They had nodded to each other but Blister was with his pals and they were concentrating on the dart board. Cedric drank steadily, watching the arrows thud between the wires, still numb from the throttled unhappiness of that encounter with Josh, hungry but not appeasing it, desperate with no way of coping with it. A tired middle-aged man sitting in the corner of a small-town pub, beset by an inward weeping of tears he could not staunch. He missed the winks and nudges of Blister to his pals and looked up as they came to sit with him in grateful expectation; at least he would not have this hour alone.

Affairs were not going well between Blister and Maureen; there was much she regretted and he felt that, keenly. There was much he found irksome and he needed someone to turn on for relief.

'Well now, Cedric, how about setting them up!'

Cedric did not mind being asked to buy a round. You often so bought your way into a company. He went to the bar and brought over the pints himself. It was near closing time. Blister had been drinking all evening.

'What's that, Cedric?' He pointed to the pint. 'Did I say I wanted a pint?'

'I thought that was your drink.'

'Not at this time of night. I'll have a whisky. Scotch on the rocks. A Bell's.'

Cedric smiled nervously; an immense wave of weary apprehension broke through him.

'OK, Blister.'

'What did you call me?'

'What?' Cedric's fear was so plain that it goaded this man on. Blister could sense that he was isolating himself from the general sympathy and this was added fuel.

'My name? Friends call me one thing. Everybody else—' he sought for a conclusion, 'waits.'

'Sorry.' Cedric walked over. 'Here's your Scotch. It's a Bell's.'

'Arseholes!' said Blister as he tipped up the glass, 'or Bottoms Up as you navy fellas say.'

'We generally just say cheers or good luck,' Cedric sat down for fear of the consequences of walking right out as he wanted to do. 'They say different things in different countries.'

'Isn't that fantastic! What a bloody well-travelled man you have to be to say a thing like that, eh lads? Us poor sods stuck here all our naturals would never know a thing like that now, would we? How could we?'

Cedric was silent. How often had he been baited like this in the Army and on board ship! How he had dreaded it. Ullaby had been a sanctuary from that, his short passages there a rest from this masculine world in which he had always found himself, which drew him on and besotted him only to turn on him for no reason at all that he could ever see. He wanted no trouble. Even now, he did not dislike Blister—could have been friends with him, not real mates, but friendly.

'And how's the darling of Ullaby? How's your friend? Eh? You should be grateful to me for taking her away from him, eh? You owed me that whisky. You can buy yourself a motor-bike and play cops and robbers, you two. Hey! You should see them.' Blister was talking himself into an understanding of what he had not really clarified in his mind before. 'I didn't know whether Maureen was married to him or this old woman here was the wife. Hanging about like a kid, he was. I used to ask Maureen "Did he knock on the door and ask if our Josh was coming out to play?" Makes you sick!'

Blister's friends were glistening in anticipation. Behind the bar, the landlord flexed himself and weighed up the possibilities. All other talk, even the pretence of talk, ceased as the bludgeoning taunts went on. Strangely, Blister scarcely looked at his man; usually you held his eyes in the grip of a gaze—but this venom was directed at the glass and the disturbance he caused others was at least partly matched by the disturbance he was bringing on himself.

'Nancy boy! All you arseholes are the same. Hey! He used to train Josh—anybody remember that—eh? Used to make the soft bastard wear a pair of shorts and think he was some soddin' trainer, shouting at him—stupid bugger.' He did look up now, but Cedric's frightened eyes saw sufficient evidence of a similar fear in the apparently vicious glance that there was some rise of confidence in him. 'What the hell do you want here, anyway, Tyson? Piss off back to Ullaby. Go and tuck him up in his rotten bed. Nancy!'

Cedric stood up—the movement, slow, determined to be inoffensive.

'There's no need for that,' he said, throat dry, voice unsteady, only just able to contain the drumming of his heart and the reverberations of fear. He had been in this situation before and once been badly beaten; the visual remembrance of himself moaning in the gutter, his own blood mingling with the sewage of that foreign city, gave him some extra strength here. It could not be worse—and he had to speak out! Where else would he have? If this territory were to deny him, where could he go?

'I'm not setting myself up for a fight because I know you would win and I see no sense in being hammered just for a mouthful of filth like that.' Blister's head jerked back at the word 'filth'. 'I needn't deny something as wrong as what you've just said because there's no need. Josh and me got on well together. We were mates just like your lot are mates—there's never been anything against that. Anyway,' his own words encouraged him: he was still on his feet, he was being listened to—and now sorrow for his excess that morning broke through. Perhaps this would be reported back to Josh and would somehow make it quits. 'Josh is a good man, a man nobody could take against. There isn't a word could be brought against him by anybody, round here or anywhere else. I tell you. I'm glad to have somebody like that for a mate. He's worth more than anybody else I've come across wherever I've been. He's out on his own, Josh. And there's no shame in that. I trained him because he's a natural athlete. He could've excelled in whatever he'd taken on. As for me calling on him and Maureen—that's not true. I've not been back home long enough—it was you were calling on *her*.'

'Get out.' Blister's voice was peremptory. 'Get.'

'I will. But what you said was wrong.'

'Out!' He was now, truly, having difficulty in holding himself back. Cedric's early concession to his physical superiority had drawn the sting but the references to Maureen and himself had pressed it back into him.

The landlord quietly lifted the hatch and prepared to separate them.

'I'll go,' said Cedric. 'I've had my say.'

He had brought gloves and a scarf with him and one of the gloves had slipped off the seat and on to the floor. Picking it up entailed kneeling down in front of Blister who could no longer restrain himself; but he was aware of the approaching landlord and this the only decent pub in town he was allowed to drink in, aware, too, of a feeling of pity for Cedric's self-proclaimed weakness and of some justice in the man's defence. His action, then, though designed to hurt was not that blind-minded lashing out with which he usually attempted to obliterate his enemies.

He grabbed Cedric's hair, above the forehead, on the thatched part, grasped it hard and tight. Cedric froze—struggle, he knew, would have terrible consequences. 'Let him *be*, Blister,' the landlord was up beside him, as high above Blister as Blister was above Cedric.

'The bugger's not scratchin' about between *my* legs.' At pains to justify himself, Blister used a jibe whose unfairness was clearly felt by all, himself included.

'Up,' he said. 'Up.' Blister began to get to his feet: Cedric's sole concern was to match his rise.

'Blister! I'm warning you. You'll have no more drink in this house if there's trouble. Let him alone.'

'You grab a dog by its scruff, don't you? Eh? Up! Up!'

Cedric's hands were raised beside his ears, hovering in support of the specially plaited wig.

To finish this distastefully one-sided contest as quickly as possible, Blister yanked hard at Cedric, intending to make him wince and then let go. His hand held on to a chunk of hair. Instantly, Blister saw the chance of resolving all the sickly confusions of this business—'Baldy!' he shouted. His hand struck again, ripping out another patch of hair.

'Bald as a bloody egg! Well—you great big daft old tart!'

Cedric covered his face with his hands and they left him alone.

So Blister was already worked up when he arrived back at Beth's that night. Beth herself was in bed—with a headache, so she had said—and Jack decided to join her when he saw the hard look on Blister. Maureen had not acknowledged his entrance, fixing her attention yet more firmly on the television. He dumped himself into the settee beside her.

'Good night all.' Jack bounced up as Blister went down; they might have been at opposite ends of the same see-saw. 'Be good.'

There was no response to this humorous parting shot.

'How about a drop of tea then,' Blister was not entertained by the film of Pacific Islanders placidly enacting obscure erotic rituals.

'You know where to find it.'

One reply, one sentence only and he was on edge—yet he was also caught by her. No one had ever answered him back with such casual fearlessness; no one made him feel so bad and yet, as a sort of spice to it all, feel so bad not only in the sense of inferior but wicked. He wanted to embrace her and hurt her at once, to pierce her, causing them both pleasure and herself pain. Since living with her, his desire had grown wilder and was now feeling the first chill of despair as she began to make her doubts and aversions more obvious.

'Cedric's bald,' he said, after a pause to digest the gob of temper. 'He is! Bald as a coot!'

Maureen looked at him and grinned, happily. 'Really!' She laughed. 'God, that's a laugh.'

'He looks about seventy without his hair—he does. He'd had it stitched in or something like that. You could tell by looking at its roots.'

'When was this?'

'Just now. In The Lion and Lamb.'

'Did he—he wouldn't tell you—how did you find out?'

'Oh—me and him had a, you know—nothing much—I wasn't barred or anything. This thing of his came away in my hand.'

'You mean you ripped it off the poor fella's head.'

'Like a bloody Indian with a scalp, I was.'

'What had he done to bother you?'

'Nothing.'

'What was it?'

'I've said. Nothing.'

'You got at him to get at Josh, didn't you, that was it, wasn't it? Just like when you threatened that other Ullaby lot on Saturday night. That's it, isn't it? You can't leave it alone, can you?'

'Get us some tea, Maureen, eh? Will you?'

'Yes.' To confuse and surprise him she got up.

While she was out he switched programmes on the television. None of them interested him. He knocked it off and put on the wireless. The sudden loud sound of pop was immediately followed by banging on the ceiling. He grinned at the annoyance he was causing.

'If you don't turn that down you'll have our Beth down and I've had enough of her for one fine day thank you very much, so turn it down.'

'She's getting on your nerves then, is she?' Blister disguised his defeat (he turned down the volume) by this uncustomary concern.

'Everybody's bound to get on everybody's nerves jumbled up like we are.'

'We could go to my mother's.'

'And have my head chewed off?'

'I'll get a place.'

'Nobody'll give us a place without being married.'

'What's wrong with this?'

'It's too crowded and I'm sick of Beth's filthy language. Half of it's only to impress you.'

'What makes you say that?' Blister was flattered, knowing that Beth fancied him; he flirted with her.

'Oh don't pretend. You make me sick the way the pair of you play up to each other. If you knew what fools you looked!'

'I like it here—and that's enough lip. I let you go a long way but nobody walks all over me. Understand?'

'I wish you would stop imitating some cowboy. Honestly—

sometimes I think you lot wouldn't know how to go about things if it wasn't for cowboy pictures. You carry on just like them.'

'Just because I told you all them facts about the West.'

Blister had scrimmaged his way through a few paperbacks and magazine articles on this his tepidly pursued hobby; he considered himself a man of some learning in the subject. 'There's no need to throw them in my face. You would be a bloody sight better off for a job, you. It would keep your mind occupied and bring a bob or two in that we could use.'

'I knew you'd be on to that.'

'OK. So shut up.'

'I'll work when I feel like it.'

'I know. OK.'

'And if it hurts you to put your hand in your pocket you know what you can do.'

'O . . . K!'

'It's bad enough shopping with everybody bloody well staring at you. "There she is—leaving her kid"—all those hypocritical old bags that nearly drive their husbands cracked by rationing the sex and worshipping the rotten advertisements.'

'How do you know?'

'They look like it. My God! I used to dream that Thurston was a hive of activity when I was stuck up in those mountains. But I might as well be back there for all the life *we* get.'

'Go back then.'

'I might.'

There was no way of telling whether or not her reply was merely bravado. She did not know herself.

'Anyway! I want to see Anne again. I miss her. It's only natural. I'm going back to see her.'

Out of the silence which succeeded this over-vehement statement, Blister gained an accurate insight and spoke to it.

'Josh's the one you want to see,' he said, evenly. 'Don't try to kid me. But listen, Maureen, no, don't pretend to read that bloody thing!' He leapt across to her and ripped the magazine from between her hands, standing above her in a cold rage. 'If you try it out on me—you're in trouble. And, listen again—listen,' he grabbed her wrist fiercely. 'Have anything more to do with him and I'll do him. I will. I'll smash the sod. Husband or no husband.'

Maureen pulled hard and he released her. She, too, came to her feet and looked at him without flinching. 'You touch him, Blister—just touch him—and we're finished. Completely finished.'

Cedric shivered in his bed. He could not curse them: he could not get them. He was afraid and cold and desolate.

CHAPTER EIGHTEEN

THE Huntsman walked into the village just before eight, heavy boots, dark brown breeches, scarlet coat and waistcoat, black velvet hat, white shirt and a boyish tie, red, with yellow horse-shoes on it. Around him were the hounds, either jogging sedately in the middle of the road as a pack or slouchily galloping off to some smell in a hedge or lane. The whipper-in snapped instructions at these loners, exercising the controls he would have to apply through the day. Dressed like his superior, he was distinguished by a large leather pouch which swung at his hips; he enjoyed banging against it, as he did, at every step. The Huntsman was a much less excited man, though he would have liked a village clock to strike eight as he arrived at the pub, a coincidental and timely fanfare he enjoyed in other places. It was too much to expect a clock, though, in Ullaby. There was some satisfaction, warm inside him, at the idea of Ullaby's meagre resources; jokes could be made endlessly about Ullaby; you could tack on to its inhabitants all those stories of meanness and strangeness which involved Cumbrian characters. He only gave the village a hunt because it was ideally placed in a good area of country. You would have thought a place like this would have appreciated a bit of a change, but to look around, it was ready for a funeral—if that. Only this little girl out to welcome them; flitting along beside him as if he was the leader of a band. Lovely little thing she was.

And what a day for the job! The mist was almost all cleared away—the morning would dry out fast and the scent would be strong. From here, fox could either take them into secluded, interlocking small fell-valleys which scarcely saw either tourist or local, having neither lakes nor pasture—lovely hunting country, where a man was the only thing that mattered between the ground and the sky and a fox could have a clear run; or it could make for the plain, down by Thurston or Waverton or places like that, down through the streets and round the houses—rare fun then! Then you wished you were on a horse and not just foot-hunters—but which horse could live in the fells? They could keep their horses, this was ordinary man's sport—and twice he'd ended up on the beach with a kill on the sand, the hounds at the animal while the waves broke gently nearby. That was one of the attractions of Ullaby—it could go either way.

There were a few followers outside the pub and he pulled back his shoulders a bit. More would join in throughout the day —with their cars which were very useful and promised well for the collection. The landlord was a little surly about doing the honours with the whisky bottle but the Huntsman chose to ignore it and took a very full glass.

The vicar moved over to stand near Anne, surprised to see her out on her own. She took his hand and stared at the hounds which shifted ceaselessly about the space before the pub. Their noises, the chatter of the men, the shouted greetings and commands—it was as if a carnival had burst on to her tranquil playground of a village.

'*You* have her.' Josh came up to him; he could not conceal his relief. He picked her up and hugged her. 'I thought you were just outside in the garden, you silly old black puddin'.'

She giggled. 'You are—you're a black puddin' for running away from Daddy like that. And who didn't finish her breakfast, eh?'

'Me. Anne. I didn't.' Again she giggled, realizing her mischievousness. 'Daddy? Are those dogs going to eat somebody?'

'Don't be daft.' He kissed her, pretending it was to calm her fear, but she was not afraid.

'Why are they like that then?'

'They're going to hunt. They're going to catch foxes.'

'And kill them?'

'Yes. Foxes are nasty beasts, you know. They kill sheep and

hens—and chickens; they kill chickens.'

'Why do they?'

'Because they want something to eat and they don't know any better.'

'Poor foxes.'

'Once upon a time,' chanted the vicar 'there were three little foxes; and they didn't wear trousies and they didn't wear sockses; but they all dum de dum dum, something, something, something; and kept their handkerchiefs in cardboard boxes!'

'Josh!' The whipper-in, who liked to recognize people he knew before a hunt, liked to see his acquaintanceship broadcast over the county, laid a strong hand on Josh's shoulder and nodded at Anne.

'Alec!' Josh blushed a little, being singled out. 'I'd heard you were a whipper-in.'

'Yours?' Alec nodded and included Annie in the nod.

'Yes.'

'A once-offer? Or is there a crop?'

'Just her.'

'Would you like to pat the best hound in Cumberland?' he asked the little girl.

Anne looked at Josh and then reached out her arms to the whipper-in. Surprised at her willingness, but very pleased, he took her and walked through the pack, pushing through them as a man pushes through water, the pouch bouncing against his thigh.

'Alec Stainton,' Josh explained to the vicar. 'He used to play for us at football.'

'It's sad how easily men can be brought together for death,' said the vicar, expressing a line of thought he had been privately following up all the while. 'Would they celebrate a birth with as much enthusiasm? Would they all run up a mountain to see the birth of a lamb?'

'They see that every day,' Josh answered, shyly.

'They eat meat every day, too. No—they want to be in at a kill. In this place, Josh, I clearly remember being told by those who had no need to lie, from this peaceful little village, men marched away to war in 1914 as if they'd been off to an outing or a fair. It's a great thing to civilize such terrible destructiveness. Doing that is worth a thousand churches, however beautiful.'

He had left his listener way behind and, realizing it, stopped. 'You look so *well*, Josh,' he said. 'So much happier. It's a sad commentary on poor Maureen, but you look younger, too, keener, like you used to.'

'It's with everything being in the open. That's a big help, you know.'

'I saw her the other evening. She looks well, too. But perhaps looks are not even superficially useful. She must miss her daughter a great deal. I still believe you were wrong to separate them.'

'I know you do.'

'No one is that much in the right. It must seem to her that you made a choice between them.'

'She's welcome back any day, any hour. You can't be fairer than that.'

'Sometimes our propositions seem so kind to us and are so cruel to others. You could help her more, Josh. You could talk to her.'

Josh moved away and the vicar let him go: he had unsettled the young man enough.

'Norman's coming out after we've milked,' said Josh to Alec. 'In fact, he's hoping to be in near the start.'

'Has he paid his subscription then?' The young whipper-in was already learned in the old jokes and taunts; he would soon be a huntsman in his own right, this one.

'Don't bring that up.' Josh spoke earnestly. 'He was never done talking about that—it upset me as much as him in the end. He's no less than honest, Norman. You couldn't have a straighter man than him.'

'You bloody Ullaby clan stick together!' Alec beamed and handed Anne over to him. 'Here's a parcel for Christmas.'

'Can *I* go, Daddy?'

'Aye, bring her,' encouraged Alec who was taken with the child. 'She'll enjoy all the shouting and that.'

'Please. Please.'

Josh was not fond of hunts; without drawing attention to his aversion he would avoid them. But Alec's invitation was so warm and Anne tugged at him so pleadingly.

'I'll see, after dinner, eh? I could take a sandwich for me dinner and have the afternoon. Wilson would probably see his way to it; we're just making work for ourselves as it is.'

'We'll not be far off. We're drawing Dial End for a start-off. You'll hear us, anyway, if the hunt's worth a damn. Away now!' He had caught the Huntsman's eye and observed the small horn being slipped out of the pocket. 'Away! Away! Away!'

The horn was blown, the dogs moved off, and the Huntsman ordered them out of the village on the west side, up to the small wood known as Dial End.

In the single-decker bus which brought her out of Thurston, Maureen sat at the back though most of the seats were unoccupied and it was unusual for a woman travelling alone to sit in so isolated a seat. It was unmistakable that she wanted to be on her own and the young conductor was intrigued by that. He kept glancing at her, even staring at her, until she concentrated on looking out of the window and ignored him. Things were too serious for even the lightest diversions.

Some men were taking the road up just beyond Brindlefield, laying a new surface, Blister's clique were among them. They saw her plainly and nudged each other. So he would be told soon. He worked on another road-gang but they were bound to meet up in the day, sooner rather than later if she could judge from the interest she had so quickly aroused.

The bus was marked ULLABY.

It took its time to get there, acting, really, as a roundabout taxi for the women who by day were isolated in small cottages and hamlets all over the district. It took its time to get there and once the driver slowed down to a crawl to watch the hunt moving along a ridge of fell. Strung out, the men were, well into the morning now, raincoats flying in the wind, the yelping of dogs clear on the hillside, the procession looked endless; black cut-out figures on the skyline.

She shivered when the bus gathered speed once more. In a few minutes she would be in her own house.

He sat in front of the mirror looking at the effect. He had

found two hats—a brown trilby and an old-fashioned cap. Neither looked well on him. At this moment, he was examining the cap. It was just that little bit too small. He tugged it, then pushed it towards one ear, slid it back and brought it forward.

It was terrible but it was better than the trilby. He had tried to cover the bare patches but without success. He took off the cap now and looked at the damage. It looked worse than a really bald man, somehow. He replaced the cap. He would go into Carlisle that day and get a decent cap. It would be a waste of time and money getting it re-thatched. Everybody would know and so for the moment the best thing was to conceal it as many other balding men did.

There was no doubt that he would be a laughing-stock for some time to come. As far as he could imagine, he would be persecuted by many delighted to have such an opportunity.

He had bought a knife in some forgotten foreign part. A flick knife with a gaudily ornamented handle. He took it up now and pointed it at himself in the mirror. 'If they come near me they'll get *that*!' he said, and the blade jumped out.

In folding it up and slipping it into his side-pocket there was some satisfaction; the edge was taken off his defencelessness, it was an antidote to the hopelessness of spirit he felt after so many defeats on the previous day.

He went out and down the village towards the bus stop. The single-decker came up from Thurston once in the morning, once in the late afternoon. At Thurston he could make a connection for Carlisle where there would be a wide range of hats and he could choose without being observed.

'I've never heard the like! A little thing like that running about with great soft men running about after a poor little fox! Get away with you, Josh Lawton! She'll stay with me and have a good hot meal and half an hour's rest after it, that's what she'll do. You go away if you want—but don't try to use her for an excuse. Take a child on a foxhunt indeed! It's not even as if you have a car to give her little legs a rest. She'll turn into no savage while I'm keeping an eye on her and that's a fact you'll have to lump, Josh Lawton. I'm *surprised* at you! Now you come here, pet, and you be away with those swearing men running after wild animals and just as bad themselves. No—there's no use in pulling and tugging, my fine lady, you're going to be washed and cleaned up for your dinner. And your father can take his sandwiches and depart.'

Mrs Wilson drew Anne in through the back door and banged it, hard. It was so rarely there arose the opportunity of scolding Josh with good cause; she had seized it gladly and enjoyed it.

Alone in the farmyard, Josh turned away feeling very half-hearted about going to the hunt, but he was commited to it now. It would not do to hang around and say he did not want to go; that would be like sulking; like playing a game only if he got his own way.

He went towards his cottage land and, about half-way there, found Cedric waiting for him.

'I'm sorry about losing my temper yesterday.'

'That's all right.' Josh was much more uncomfortable than his friend.

'No but I'm sorry.'

'You were worked up a bit, that's all.'

'Start again then? Eh? Cedric held out his hand. Josh was forced to take it but the grip was not hearty.

'I was going home to pick up the bike and have a look out for that hunt.'

'No need for your bike, man—no! It's only over at Crozier's—that new bus conductor had seen it—he told me. We'll be far better off walking along past Routledge's and meeting them at Fall Tarn—you can't get a bike up there and we can always cadge a lift if there's a chase.'

His argument was sound and Josh fell in with the plan. Cedric had seen Maureen get off the bus and he had instantly decided to see Josh before she did, to re-establish himself before they met, to be certain of some affection at least.

The place was so clean. There were fresh flowers in a vase on the mantelpiece. It was so peaceful. She had turned on the wireless on coming in but soon she turned it off again, to appreciate the silence.

The bed had not been made and she was glad to make it, tucking in the sheets as anxiously as she had done in the first months of her marriage. He had painted the bedroom white, which was unusual; the landing, too, was white.

She had heard that Anne spent the days up at Mrs Wilson's and knew that Josh had his midday meal there. She would wait until after that to go up. When Anne had a good dinner inside her and Josh was out away from the farmhouse.

Sipping at a cup of coffee, she settled in one of the armchairs and took up a magazine, still glancing around occasionally, as a visitor might; one who is impressed and pleased and would like what she sees for herself.

'There's the bloody canniest old vixen this side of Timbuctoo leading us by the nose, old lad,' said Alec, even more important in his excitement. Josh listened intently. 'I tell you—if we can winkle her out it'll be a gallop and a bloody half in a corkscrew and a bloody spiral, if you get my meaning. She won't go straight and she won't go predictable. She'll jump as she fancies and there'll be no guessing which. I tell you, it's some lovely bloody animal we're on to this day. You should've brought your little lass—what? She'd've loved all this, man. Kids lap up these sort of doings—lap them up!'

Having spoken, Alec moved on, to moderate his enthusiasm in the company of a group of heavy-faced, raw-cheeked farmers and labourers who were discussing the fox's genius and combining in an attempt to outwit it. Norman was with them. He was disappointed that Josh stuck with Cedric and simultaneously annoyed that Cedric would not leave Josh's side. It was less aggravating in the circumstances to be on his own. The hounds were in disarray and the Huntsman motioned to Alec to call them together until they should have worked out a plan. Alec hurled their names into the air and the fells sang with these old appellations, handed down from hound to hound as strictly as a surname. 'Bellman!' 'Ranter.' 'Royal.' 'True!' 'True'—that was 'the best hound in Cumberland' whose ears Anne had tickled at the morning meet.

Cedric and Josh had soon caught the quality of the occasion. In no time Cedric was giving his opinion and, conscious of impressing Josh as he always had done when he had dominated a conversation, he became less apprehensive and even grew quite animated.

'She'll be bound to have gone over water to lose a pack of hounds, now there can't be two ways about that. I mean, we can argue it out but there isn't any question, the only means a fox has for breaking its scent is water and that's above all contradiction. Now wait—wait—there must be some sort of a beck in that bit of a wood. I *know* you say there isn't but funnier things have happened than underground streams suddenly springing up. I mean, they're there all the effing rotten time, they've got to spring up some day of the week. And she'll have padded up it—now you can say what you want. Just find the water and you'll get to the effing animal. Mind; if she's as clever as you've painted her—she could be in Scotland by now.'

It was decided to drag the wood.

As he went between the trees, ahead of him the hounds baying at the air, around him the dialect he had heard all his life and nearby the place and the child he loved most in the world, Josh had a great feeling of happiness; just being in such good company on such a fine fresh day—here, in the open, where your mind was blown clean of all worries if you could believe hard enough. He felt it would all work out—Maureen, Annie and himself—it would all be good again if he wanted it enough.

'Bellman! Ranter! Royal! True! Away! Away!'

Mrs Wilson handed over Anne's coat under silent protest. That the little girl clung around her mother's neck did not move her to any sympathy for this faithless woman. It was only, as she was to say immediately afterwards to Mr Wilson, 'It was only for the child's sake that I tolerated her coming into the kitchen at all.'

They played hide-and-seek on the way back home. Annie had not yet quite understood the game or perhaps she enjoyed her own version too much to abandon it. 'Hiding' for her consisted in standing still and covering up her eyes: when Maureen came up to her and said 'Boo!'—Anne would pretend to tremble and then say 'Now you hide—but don't go away!' meaning—keep in sight.

Maureen was thankful that they met no one on the way to the cottage. Word would be around the village and everyone would know—but it was a relief not to have to encounter people. Mrs Wilson had, for her, typified the reaction she expected from this secretive and censorious little community.

Just before they went in, the hunt came into view up beyond the quarry, moving along a rim of it back towards Dial End where they had made the first draw.

'They're all going to kill a fox,' said Anne, proud of her knowledge. 'Because a fox kills chickens.'

The vixen they were pursuing would be found to have a crippled foreleg. She had once before been hunted just as closely as on this day and at that time had leapt on to a wall which was crested by barbed wire. Getting through it had ripped the leg open and the lamed, bleeding animal would have been easy meat: but the dogs were driven back by the wire and by the time the Huntsman had come up to direct them to other routes, she had been safely away.

She had begun to play the two woods in order to confine the pack while her cubs ran free and away from the dogs. But the pursuit had been hard, her evasions more exhausting than she could easily bear. She had not the energy to break for open countryside and yet the longer she kept in this limited area the more the hounds would learn of the tracks, the more the men would see her plans; she would be cornered.

In the small intimately-known space, the exictement of the men intensified. Usually they were spread out over miles of empty land; on this day they circled the same territory, dragging it, using it, land so close to their homes that they knew each small hillock and fence, had shot there and run there, farmed and played there all their lives. Names of fields and hedges in this confined area, were as well-known as the grander names of fells which marked other hunts. This was indeed Ullaby's Meet.

Josh forgot himself. Never far from the front, he raced across screes to catch up with the hounds, and slithered down the hillside, his face illuminated with pleasure as the men he had so long known fed their concentrated desire into this chase.

Some of them began to shout; yelps more than shouts they were, not unlike the crying of the hounds. And in the sport Josh saw with intense pleasure the delight of Norman and Alec and others he knew; their mood blessed his own. And Cedric, too, was like his old self.

So on the fellside above the fell village the men hounded their prey; below, people in the cottages heard and prepared to go out to see the sport; and below the village, those on the plain looked up at the hills and thought them bare and silent.

The vicar had dozed in the large armchair by the fire as he often did. On his lap was *King Solomon's Mines*, one of his favourites that he read again and again.

He woke up and saw it was the middle of the day. The fire was out. He looked around his cluttered, crowded room, stuffed with school photographs, college photographs, photographs of relatives and youthful friends—and everywhere, snaps of the Boys he had fathered. The furniture was comfortable, Victorian, substantial, too big and too grand for the cottage. Every article in the house had known a place in his mind and its associations could touch his heart. But the things were not enough.

In the small kitchen he ate a lump of cheese and some Ryvita biscuits. To warm up he had a powerfully strong mug of instant coffee, heavily sweetened. He unlatched the back door and looked out across to the fells, soon catching the sound of the pack.

Tired and troubled, the good old man went into his bedroom and knelt beside the large bed, his hands clasped before his face in the manner children use.

'Our Father,' he began, and repeated the Lord's prayer as he did every day before going to his bed. And all the time the sound of the pack which grew with his imaginings.

'Dear Lord,' he said, when he had finished the prescribed prayers. 'Help me to be strong in my dealings with Josh. I taught him Your ways and he believed. I see his soul in his eyes and it is in danger. I pester him too much, I know, and I confuse him with my talk which is always serious. I cannot be at ease with him, O Lord. His virtue as a boy struck me with awe and even now, when he is sadly mistaken, I run to him to see the working of Your grace. Let me not press him further. Let my spirit not come between him and You. Let me leave him to Your safe-keeping who guards us all, through Jesus Christ, Thy only beloved Son, who for our sake came down from Heaven, and was made flesh. Amen.'

Seeing the excitement, some of the quarrymen had knocked off early and come up to join the hunt followers, now an intent pack, for the vixen had been seen to slip across to Dial End and been observed to be very big and very tired. The kill of such a prey would be worth the attendance.

One of these men was Bobbie Calthwaite who had brought Duke along with him. He tagged on to Josh and Cedric, Cedric high with anticipation, imagining this hunt to be a hunt for all manner of enemies, the fells a terrain perilous and threat-infested, himself and Josh true heroes among the commoners, himself the great saviour, soon to be revealed when he risked his own life to rescue his loyal friend from the very jaws of death. It was such a pleasure to bask once more in these lurid fantasies—they had always needed some real concrete analogy, however slight, in order to function properly and the reunion with Josh on such a hunt as this was more than sufficient for his purpose.

'I *said* she'd have slipped over to Dial, didn't I? Didn't I? I said that, didn't I? And who mentioned that gully? Not as a gully but as water, eh? See? You can learn a thing or two when you're on your own on these initiative tests they used to send us on. Dropped in the middle of nowhere with two days' rations and about five bob—and they were iron rations, I can tell you—and a compass. You haven't *lived*. I can tell you What? And if she's tired, she'll trail around that effing wood till she has that pack sniffing up their own backsides!'

'She's looking well anyway,' said Bobbie, heartily, to Josh. He had been home for his dinner and heard that Maureen was in the village. He spoke to reassure Josh, to tell him that he, Bob Calthwaite, was honestly pleased that Maureen was back and wasn't going to say anything or hold anything against her.

'We'll have to step out to catch them up—come on!' Cedric moved ahead, afraid now of the results of his concealment.

'You saw her, didn't you, Cedric? My missis said you were near the bus-stop when she got off.'

Cedric ignored him.

'Well,' Bobbie concluded, 'it'll be nice for the little girl to see her mother, won't it? They all miss their mammies, whatever you say.'

'Maureen's back?'

'You didn't know?'

'In Ullaby?' Josh felt his heart lift, physically it felt as if his heart actually jumped inside his body and the blood raced round so fast he was momentarily dizzy.

'Cedric must have told you.'

'No.' Josh turned to go. 'Thanks,' he said, and began to run at first slowly and then, as the realization cleared, faster and faster down the hill towards the village.

Cedric stood very still. Josh had not looked at him: not even a reproachful glance—no recognition, none. Yet to that tart he now ran, leaping down the fellside swiftly, intently. Bob Calthwaite grinned at Cedric, knowingly, but the taunt was absorbed in the blankness and there was no time now to tease, the hounds were curdling the air with the longing in their howls.

It was a very strange sensation. As if he were crying, inside himself; as if the fleshy underskin were weeping into his body, from all its scarlet glistening surface; and then the weeping grew stronger and the shell of himself liquefied. He stood, watching Josh go down, and felt himself drained with the fear of loss.

The men had moved on and he was alone.

As soon as he came through the door, she put her fingers to her lips and smiled. He glanced across at Anne, stretched out fast asleep on the settee, her face white as it always was in sleep, lips parted and long lashes not quite covering that small gap between the eyelids. Josh always wanted to put his thumbs on them and gently close them, tight shut. He did so now, to ease this meeting.

The wireless was playing, softly, the record 'My Sweet Lord' by George Harrison. The gentle, earnest sweetness of words and music helped, like the sleeping child, to give the first awkward moments some tenderness. They spoke quietly, near a whisper.

'She just went out like a light,' said Maureen. 'One minute she was full of herself and the next she was sucking her thumb and gone.'

Josh nodded, as if he had heard of a marvellous accomplishment. He took off his cap, came across the room and sat in his usual seat opposite her. Together they looked over at the child and, as if addressing Anne, Josh said:

'It's grand to see you back, Maureen. We've been . . . missing you; badly. Missing you.'

'I don't know,' her tone was pert, her expression amused, 'it seems to me you've been doing very well for yourself. Whose idea was it to paint the bedroom?'

'I thought,' Josh put his hand to his mouth to quell a cough, 'I wanted to sort of freshen it up a bit and white seemed the best way. It's easy to paint over if you don't like it.'

'Oh no. It's nice. A bit cold for my liking, but . . .' She wanted to keep up banter. She felt that this return had clarified a decision but she wanted to avoid confronting it.

'I love that song,' she said and began to sing, murmuring to herself ' "Really want to see you; Really want to see you: Really want to see you; Really want to see you: Really want to see you Lord." I keep meaning to buy it.'

Josh smiled and put his hands behind his head, locking his fingers to provide a headrest; steadying himself, almost bracing himself.

'It's good to see that chair full again.' He laughed when he saw the wry reception she gave his remark. 'You know what I mean.'

'Has she been good?'

'She's asked after you a lot.'

'What did you say?'

'You were on holiday, I said. You'd gone for a rest.'

'Maybe that's true.'

'Well you're back now anyway.'

Maureen wanted to say, 'Is that all? You want it so easily wrapped up. Is that all you can say? I am here but I will not stay. You *could* talk to me, you could help me to be persuaded, you could force me, you could blackmail me with Anne, you could cry and I would stay. You could do something that would let us be together as two people and not me on my knees before your image and you on your knees before my image and neither of us out in the real world, spellbound by this altar we've put before ourselves. There are more pieces in the puzzle than two. We *aren't* going to live happily ever after, Josh. I love you, I love you, I'll always love you and no one in the world I'll meet will come near you or harm you in my mind but I can't stand this closed-in life any more. Not just in here or in Ullaby, though even that, though I love it for a change, I couldn't really have again—but you're being so nice and lovely and good to me and never wrong—it makes me want to bury my head for shame. And nothing seems to affect you, none of the little things, none of the ordinary gossip and rows and chat and stuff —you can live without that. I can't. Silly reasons as well as big reasons, Josh, my love, Josh. But I cannot live with you. The case is packed with Annie's clothes and a few toys and we'll go away. It'll hurt you—but I must have her. However bad a mother, I'm still a mother and will be. I'm sorry. I'm so sorry, Josh.'

He sought comfort and reassurance in the silence and, as unaware of her decisions as he was of her dismay at his words, he said: 'I always knew it would come out right. There's nobody like you, Maureen. I always knew it would be all right again between us two if only I waited. I didn't mind how long I waited. I knew it would work out.'

Maureen was very near to crying but forced herself to check it. There he sat, just a few feet away—it could have been a ravine which separated them. So lovely, he looked—she used the feminine word without it troubling her now; once she would have defended him vigorously against such a womanly description but it came easily—still the sweet face, unworn, even the pulling silence of these last few months together vanished—he did look better without her—and so gentle, manly, kind; but though she could admire him she was afraid in some way. All the time in the cottage she had seen them together again—and his silences which seemed so restful appeared chill; his concern which seemed so amiable was irksome; his love which had seemed so complete was not able to move her. 'I think, Josh, that I won't be staying.'

He did not reply.

'I'm sorry.'

He looked to one side of her and then his eyes moved over to Anne.

'We'll have to wait a bit longer then.'

'Yes.'

She got up. There was no point in saying more, in stating what would become obvious. She went across to Anne and shook her lightly on the shoulder.

'Mammy,' a thin arm went around Maureen's neck and she felt her mouth fill with sobs which had to be forced back. 'Mammy, Mammy. Look! There's Daddy!' She beckoned but Josh could not go over; could not trust himself that far.

Maureen stood up with Anne in her arms. She had not the courage to say the next thing directly to Josh though it was meant for him.

'I've put all your nicest dresses in a case; and Teddy and Panda and Elizabeth and that little wagon. We're going to stay with Auntie Beth for a bit.'

'All of us?'

'Just you and me.'

'For a holiday.'

'Yes.'

'Goody! Goody!' Anne kissed Maureen on the cheeks. 'I'll love a holiday, won't I?'

When she did look over at Josh, she saw that he was frightened. She felt exhausted by it all and wished it over.

Blister came into the village as the hunt moved into the top of the wood on what was to be the decisive draw. He drew up some distance from the cottage and watched them as he walked from his car to the house. The proximity of the event had drawn people out of their houses and many from the village were gazing up the fell, above the quarry, knowing that a drive downwards must bring the fox very near the village itself.

Cedric saw him go to their door. He had followed Josh down and been waiting outside since. He feared that he had utterly failed his friend by the deceit and he fingered the knife, nervously.

The door opened and as if she had been fully expecting him, Maureen soon appeared, Anne in her arms, Blister given a case to carry. Her coat was open and Anne had tugged off one of the buttons of her blouse; the breasts were seen white above the cups. Cedric could not bear to stand aside any longer.

'What about Josh?' he shouted. 'You can't leave him on his own without the little girl. Josh! Josh!'

Josh came to the doorway.

'Shut your bloody rotten mouth!' Blister had come looking for a fight and he was as prepared to go for Cedric as anybody else. 'Baldy! He's bald—did you know that?'

He turned to pass on the news to Josh, momentarily forgetting, expecting the reward of a laugh.

'Maureen,' said Josh, 'please leave Annie here.'

'Come on.' Maureen spoke equally to her daughter and her lover. 'Let's get a move on.'

'Should I carry her for you?'

'No. No—she'll be fine. Let's go to your car.'

'No.' As they moved away Josh came after them as if drawn by a cord.

'Don't let them get away with it, Josh!' Cedric's pain at his humiliation broke through. Blister was near him now and he swung out the suitcase which banged into Cedric and burst open. Clothes and toys scattered on the narrow, gravelled road.

'Pick it up!' Blister's anger with himself compounded the other tensions. 'You.' He grabbed Cedric's jacket and pushed him downwards. 'Pick it up.' Cedric went down and as he did, Blister let go the jacket and knocked off the cap, revealing the bare patched scalp.

'You go with him,' Josh spoke to Maureen as to someone with limited understanding, 'and I'll take her. Here—Annie—come to Daddy.'

'No! She'll not. Blister—help him with that case for Christ's sake. For Christ's sake we've got to go. We've got to go!' Panic was there and the child caught it immediately, began to whimper. Maureen wanted to cross herself. She longed to make the sign on her body, but was too timid in public.

'Come to Daddy. She's happy in her own house, aren't you? Eh?' He reached for her again and again Maureen stepped away, turning her back to him. Annie began to cry—the sound matching the increasing anticipation in the howls of the stalking dogs up on the fellside.

'Maureen. You can't have her.'

'Bloody well push off!' Blister came across and shoved Josh in the chest with both hands—the least hurtful blow he could strike, restrained, in his own terms, relative to the charge of the increasingly complicated pressures of anger.

'Maureen.' Her name was lifted to her so poignantly that she had to turn and face him.

'I can't, Josh. I can't.' To Blister she said. 'You. You are horrible. Horrible.'

'Anne. Annie!' Josh's eyes were full with tears as he stepped forward yet again to claim his daughter.

Blister hit him violently, high on the cheek the blow landed and the crack was as clear as the snapping of a dry branch.

Anne screamed. 'Daddy! Daddy!'

'Get him, Josh!' Cedric jumped up from the suitcase. 'Get him—you've got to or you've had it—go on, Josh!'

'You—you bald headed twat-faced prick! I'll bloody murder you.'

Cedric shouted out but before Blister could get to him, Josh was between them. He caught Blister in a wrestling grip and threw him away. Cedric had pulled out his knife but he did not open it yet, kept it in the palm.

'NO! OH NO! Please!' Maureen's cries mingled with those of Anne but both were subdued by the ferocity of the fight which followed.

Both men were strong and hard and enduring. Blister's mind was engulfed by the feeling of destructive blankness which overpowered him as if he had been injected with a powerful drug; Josh was fighting both for the life he had won and the life he had created.

People came running down the village to see it and they

would talk about the fight long after; none of them, none, could remember anything approaching it. It went along the lane, away from the cottage towards the middle of the village where there was that barn which had been a church and the yew tree which could be the oldest in the district. One of those who came was Bobbie Calthwaite's sister and Maureen gave Annie to her, asking her to take the child away from it—but poor Cissie Calthwaite, though willing and good hearted, was easily excited and curious. She only drew off a little way and ssshhed the sobbing child abstractedly while she stood on tiptoe to watch them hit each other. Blister picked his blows carefully. He realized that he could not beat Josh by any tactic of attempting to panic him or by rushing him and he contented himself with jabbing and kicking out, each hit at once a release of hatred and an excitement to greater hatred. He concentrated on Josh's face, aiming for the nose, which was soon bleeding, but more often connecting with the eyes, those sweet bemused eyes which split his knuckles and would not close. Josh was less concerned with his fists; he would try to get in close, catch Blister in a wrestling grip and throw him; then he would stand back while the other man got up. One of these blows sent Blister into the crowd and people screamed as he landed among them and they winced to see him fall so heavily and awkwardly. But he was up immediately and once more picking out savage red bruises on Josh's face. The crowd began to moan for Josh, to will him to win, to help him save himself from such disfigurement.

'Please Josh,' Cedric murmured, stalking them, never more than two yards from them, giving all his strength of will and hope to the man he loved, who had begun to fight on his account, 'oh please Josh, get him, get him, kill him, please: *hit* him Josh, use your fists, your *fists*, Josh—oh please Josh, get him, get him, go in close, close, don't let him lie there, get him, jump on him, please, please, kill him Josh.'

The breath of the two men sounded coarse and brutal, so heavy and loud it was. The crowd, too, heaved out their breath in strained support; and above them the hounds, almost on their prey, howled and howled in highest-pitched clamour.

Rid of the child, Maureen waited for a good moment.

Blister's mouth was bloodied, there was a lump on his forehead, another on his cheek. Josh, too, was bloody-faced and one of his fingernails was ripped. The fight had slowed down now, each one warier to commit himself to the effort of punching. Both men were breathing laboriously. They stood back from each other.

Maureen grabbed Blister's arm.

'If you don't stop I'll leave you. Stop!' He pushed her wearily, saving his energy for Josh who came towards him once more, Blister mistakenly thought, to take advantage of his encumbrance. On the fellside, the horn was blown: the fox had been sighted.

'Get away, Maureen.'

'No!'

'Get!'

'Stop! Oh stop!'

Afraid that he would be hindered and badly caught, Blister pulled his arm: she held on and was dragged by it. Josh came nearer. Blister lashed out at Maureen's face with his open hand and the slap cracked her as loudly as his first blow had struck Josh. She stumbled away, a finger-marked weal down her cheek.

'Oh no!' Josh groaned the words, shaking his head and letting his arm drop. 'Oh no!'

Blister hit him and Josh staggered but did not go down.

'He wasn't ready! He wasn't ready!' Seeing Josh in real trouble now, Cedric came forward, shouting, especially to the crowd, beside himself. 'He didn't have his fists up.'

Josh had been caught off balance and unprepared. He backed towards that once holy barn, at Blister's mercy entirely. He had no defence.

They said afterwards that Blister was like a 'madman', a 'lunatic', 'out of his mind'. 'So!' he kept repeating. 'So!' 'So!' '*So*!' And each time he said it he hit Josh hard on the face. Josh's eyes were closed: he swayed as he went backwards.

The hounds leapt up the fell, barking savagely; they had seen their prey and needed no scent.

'Daddy! Daddy!'

Anne had wriggled herself out of the inattentive grasp and

ran towards Josh. Hearing her voice, Josh smiled, opened his eyes slightly, stood still. Then Blister hit him the hardest blow of all. His head jolted back and rammed into one of the pointed stones which jutted from the barn wall. He stayed, pinned it could be seen, against the wall and then slithered down it.

The hushed crowd closed in on the man so obviously wounded. Anne and Cedric were beside him. Cedric took the pulse—then, terror all about him, he lifted up the arm to another. A voice said: 'O God! He's dead. Get a doctor. I think he might be dead.'

Cedric's cry was never forgotten. He went through the people he had known so long, straight for Blister, apart from all others, not yet fully realizing the fact. But though Cedric had the advantage of surprise, he was no fighter and Blister grabbed the wrist of the hand which held the knife and turned it. Cedric pushed himself on to it, Blister said later. 'I would've just held him but he rammed himself on to it: there wasn't anything I could do.'

The bodies were only a few yards apart.

The hounds scattered into the hills. After they had killed the fox they hunted in ones and twos until night.

The funerals were arranged for the following Saturday. It was much more convenient to have the one service and, though people had been uneasy when they had first heard of the idea, they came to accept it. It would have been churlish to appear divided over the matter. A local journalist had described Ullaby as a village in mourning and this phrase helped to settle and unite them. It was the vicar who had suggested the single service; his request to take it had been refused.

Maureen came with her father, and Beth came with Jack. The four of them led the procession behind the coffins and after them came two relatives of Cedric, aunts from another county; then the Wilsons. The vicar walked last.

It was hard not to cry as the coffins finally settled in the graves. The young minister's voice rose with the wind on the final words as the earth dropped lightly on to the oak. The women felt the clutch in their throats and yielded. The men, too, had to fight their emotions, and most looked away, up the fells to the empty quarry or down on to the plain, wondering, and yet already turning after so brief a time to thoughts of their own lives. Desolate, Maureen stood firm, still unable to bring the relief of tears to her stricken eyes.

Melvyn Bragg

A PLACE IN ENGLAND

What the critics said:

'A graceful and confident writer; the little Cumberland town of Thurston during the slump years, the Second World War and after, is beautifully realised, its life, rough and smooth, gathered very naturally around the central figures'

The Observer

'Since his first novel, Mr. Bragg's talent has grown until he has now achieved utter truthfulness'

The Sunday Telegraph

'An uncommonly high talent. The people are "real" enough to leave footprints right across the page'

The Guardian

'Quite masterly'

The Daily Telegraph

CORONET BOOKS

MELVYN BRAGG

SPEAK FOR ENGLAND

'A tremendous achievement—for Wigton and Mr. Bragg.'
Ray Gosling, *The Times*

'Full of humour, hope, common sense, stoicism, courage, decency . . . The voices speaking for England here are not just a collection of characters—odd, outspoken eccentric—but give a real insight into England, past and present . . . They are intelligent and individual, all sorts, all classes and condition.'
Robert Kirsch, *Los Angeles Times*

'These vivid recollections, scrupulously edited, make a book which lays plausible claim to being representative of England's history as lived and felt by her people in the twentieth century . . . The considerable pleasures and insights to be gained from the book are to be found in real memories, the measure of a life.'
Dennis Potter, *The Guardian*

'Bragg has produced a remarkable oral history . . . the hardships, the triumphs of Wigton are exhilarating, and he has recorded them with miraculous freshness and . . . deep love.'
Kirkus Reviews

CORONET BOOKS